Shoot. Whether Schoenberg was calling out the word, or he himself, or whether it only hung thought-projected in the freezing, timeless air, Suomi did not know. He knew only that death was coming for him, visible and incarnate, and his hands were good for nothing but dealing out symbols, manipulating writing instruments, paintbrushes, electronic styluses, making an impression on the world at second or third remove, and his muscles were paralyzed now and he was going to die. He could not move against the mindless certainty he saw in the thing's eyes, the certainty that he was meat . . .

BERSERKER'S PLANET

FRED SABERHAGEN

ACE SCIENCE FICTION BOOKS
NEW YORK

All characters in this book are fictitious.
Any resemblance to actual persons, living or dead,
is purely coincidental.

BERSERKER'S PLANET

Berserker's Planet was first published in *Worlds of If,* copyright © 1974
by UPD Publishing Corporation, Inc., in the June 1974 and August 1974
issues.

An Ace Science Fiction Book / published by arrangement with
the author

PRINTING HISTORY
First Ace printing / May 1980
Seventh printing / January 1986

ISBN: 0-441-05507-9

Ace Science Fiction Books are published by The Berkley Publishing Group,
200 Madison Avenue, New York, New York 10016.
PRINTED IN THE UNITED STATES OF AMERICA

I

The dead man's voice was coming live and clear over ship's radio into the *Orion*'s lounge, and the six people gathered there, the only people alive within several hundred light years, were listening attentively for the moment, some of them only because Oscar Schoenberg, who owned *Orion* and was driving her on this trip, had indicated that *he* wanted to listen. Carlos Suomi, who was ready to stand up to Schoenberg and expected to have a serious argument with him one of these days, was in this instance in perfect agreement with him. Athena Poulson, the independent one of the three women, had made no objection; Celeste Servetus, perhaps the least independent, had made a few but they meant nothing. Gustavus De La Torre and Barbara Hurtado had never, in Suomi's experience, objected to any decision made by Schoenberg.

The dead man's voice to which they listened was not recorded, only mummified by the approximately five hundred years of spacetime that stretched between Hunters' system, where the radio signal had been generated, and *Orion's* present position in intragalactic space about eleven hundred light years (or five and a half weeks by ship) from Earth. It was the voice of Johann Karlsen, who about five hundred standard years ago had led a battle fleet to Hunters' system to skirmish there with a berserker fleet and drive them off. That was some time after he had smashed the main berserker power and permanently crippled their offensive capabilities at the dark nebula called the Stone Place.

Most of the bulkhead space in the lounge was occupied by viewscreens, and then, as now, they were adjusted for the purpose, the screens brought in the stars with awesome realism. Suomi was looking in the proper direction on the screen, but from this distance of five hundred light years it was barely possible without using telescopic magnification to pick out Hunters' sun, let alone to see the comparatively minor flares of the space battle Karlsen had been fighting when he spoke the words now coming into the space yacht's lounge for Schoenberg to brood over and Suomi to record. Briefly the two men looked somewhat alike, though Suomi was smaller, probably much younger, and had a rather boyish face.

"How can you be sure that's Karlsen's voice?" Gus De La Torre, a lean and dark and somehow dangerous-looking man, asked now. He and Schoenberg were sitting in soft massive chairs facing each other across the small diameters of the lounge. The other four had positioned their

similar chairs so that the group made an approx-
imate circle.

"I've heard it before. This same sequence."
Schoenberg's voice was rather soft for such a big,
tough-looking man, but it was as decisive as usual. His gaze, like Suomi's, was on the viewscreen,
probing out among the stars as he listened intently to Karlsen. "On my last trip to Hunters',"
Schoenberg went on softly, "about fifteen standard years ago, I stopped in this region—fifteen
lights closer-in, of course—and managed to find
this same signal. I listened to these same words
and recorded some of them, just as Carlos is
doing now." He nodded in Suomi's direction.

Karlsen broke a crackling radio silence to say:
"Check the lands on that hatch if it won't seal—
should I have to tell you that?" The voice was
biting, and there was something unforgettable
about it even when the words it uttered were
only peevish scraps of jargon indistinguishable
from those spoken by the commander of any other difficult and dangerous operation.

"Listen to him," Schoenberg said. "If that's
not Karlsen, who could it be? Anyway, when I
got back to Earth after the last trip I checked
what I had recorded against historians' records
made on his flagship, and confirmed it was the
same sequence."

De La Torre made a playful tut-tutting sound.
"Oscar, did nobody ask you how you came by
your recording? You weren't supposed to be out
in this region of space then, were you, any more
than we are now?"

"Pah. Nobody pays that much attention. Interstellar Authority certainly doesn't."

Suomi had the impression that Schoenberg and De La Torre had not known each other very long or very well, but had met in some business connection and had fallen in together because of a common interest in hunting, something that few people now shared. Few people on Earth, at least, which was the home planet of everyone aboard the ship.

Karlsen said: "This is the High Commander speaking. Ring three uncover. Boarding parties, start your action sequence."

"Signal hasn't decayed much since I heard it last," Schoenberg mused. "The next fifteen lights toward Hunters' must be clean." Without moving from his chair he dialed a three-dimensional holographic astrogation chart into existence and with his lightwriter deftly added a symbol to it. The degree of clean emptiness of the space between them and their destination was of importance because, although a starship's faster-than-light translation took place outside of normal space, conditions in adjacent realms of normal space had their inescapable effects.

"There'll be a good gravitational hill to get up," said Karlsen on the radio. "Let's stay alert."

"Frankly, all this bores me," said Celeste Servetus (full figure, Oriental and black and some strain of Nordic in her ancestry, incredibly smooth taut skin beneath her silver body paint, wig of what looked like silver mist). Here lately it was Celeste's way to display flashes of insolence toward Schoenberg, to go through peri-

ods of playing what in an earlier age would have
been described as hard-to-get. Schoenberg did
not bother to look at her now. She had already
been got.

"We wouldn't be here now, probably, if it
weren't for that gentleman who's talking on the
radio." This was Barbara Hurtado. Barbara and
Celeste were much alike, both playgirls brought
along on this expedition as items for male con-
sumption, like the beer and the cigars; and they
were much different, too. Barbara, a Caucasian-
looking brunette, was as usual opaquely clothed
from knees to shoulders, and there was nothing
ethereal about her. If you saw her inert, asleep,
face immobile, and did not hear her voice or her
laugh, or behold the grace with which she
moved, you might well think her nothing beyond
the ordinary in sexual attractiveness.

Alive and in motion, she was as eye-catching
as Celeste. They were about on a par intellec-
tually, too, Suomi had decided. Barbara's remark implying that present-day interstellar human civilization owed its existence to Karlsen
and his victories over the berserkers was a
truism, not susceptible to debate or even worthy
of reply.

The berserkers, automated warships of terrible power and effectiveness, had been loosed on
the galaxy during some unknown war fought by
races long vanished before human history began.
The basic program built into all berserkers was
to seek out and destroy life, whenever and wherever they found it. In the dark centuries of their
first assaults on Earth-descended man, they had

come near overwhelming his modest dominion
among the stars. Though Karlsen and others
had turned them back, forced them away from
the center of human-dominated space, there
were still berserkers in existence and men still
fought and died against them on the frontiers of
man's little corner of the galaxy. Not around
here, though. Not for five hundred years.

"I admit his voice does something to me,"
Celeste said, shifting her position in her chair,
stretching and then curling her long naked silver
legs.

"He loses his temper in a minute here," said
Schoenberg.

"And why shouldn't he? I think men of genius
have that right." This was Athena Poulson in
her fine contralto. Despite her name, her face
showed mainly Oriental ancestry. She was better looking than nine out of ten young women,
carrying to the first decimal place what Celeste
brought to the third. Athena was now wearing a
simple one-piece suit, not much different from
what she usually wore in the office. She was one
of Schoenberg's most private and trusted secre-
taries.

Suomi, wanting to make sure he caught
Karlsen's temper-losing on his recording,
checked the little crystal cube resting on the flat
arm of his chair. He had adjusted it to screen out
conversation in the lounge and pick up only
what came in by radio. He reminded himself to
label the cube as soon as he got it back to his
stateroom; generally he forgot.

* * *

"How they must have hated him," said Barbara Hurtado, her voice now dreamy and far away.

Athena looked over. "Who? The people he lost his temper at?"

"No, those hideous machines he fought against. Oscar, you've studied it all. Tell us something about it."

Schoenberg shrugged. He seemed reluctant to talk very much on the subject although it obviously interested him. "I'd say Karlsen was a real man, and I wish I could have known him. Carlos here has perhaps studied the period more thoroughly than I have."

"Tell us, Carl," Athena said. She was sitting two chairs away. Suomi's field was the psychology of environmental design. He had been called in, some months ago, to consult with Schoenberg and Associates on the plans for a difficult new office, and there he had met Athena . . . so now he was here, on a big-game hunting expedition, of all things.

"Yes, now's your chance," De La Torre put in. Things did not generally go quite smoothly between him and Suomi, though the abrasion had not yet been bad enough to open up an acknowledged quarrel.

"Well," said Suomi thoughtfully, "in a way, you know, those machines did hate him."

"Oh no," said Athena positively, shaking her head. "Not machines."

Sometimes he felt like hitting her.

He went on: "Karlsen is supposed to have had some knack of choosing strategy they couldn't cope with, some quality of leadership . . . whatever he had, the berserkers couldn't seem to oppose him successfully. They're said to have placed a higher value on his destruction than on that of some entire planets."

"The berserkers made special assassin machines," Schoenberg offered unexpectedly. "Just to get Karlsen."

"Are you sure of that?" Suomi asked, interested. "I've run into hints of something like that, but couldn't find it definitely stated anywhere."

"Oh, yes." Schoenberg smiled faintly. "If you're trying to study the matter you can't just ask Infocenter on Earth for a printout; you have to get out and dig a little more than that."

"Why?" Infocenter, as a rule, could promptly reproduce anything that was available as reference material anywhere on Earth.

"There are still some old government censor-blocks in their data banks holding information on berserkers."

Suomi shook his head. "Why in the world?"

"Just official inertia, I suppose. Nobody wants to take the time and trouble to dig them out. If you mean why were the censor-blocks inserted in the first place, well, it was because at one time there were some people who worshipped the damned things; berserkers, I mean."

"That's hard to believe," Celeste objected. She tried to say more but was interrupted by Karlsen shouting in anger, chewing out his men about something unintelligibly technological.

"That's about the end," said Schoenberg, reaching for a control beside his chair. The frying crackle of radio static died away. "There're several hours of radio silence following." Schoenberg's eyes went shifting restlessly now to his astrogational chart. "So there was some dimwitted bureaucratic policy of restricting information about berserkers . . . the whole thing is fascinating, ladies and gents, but what say we move on toward our hunting?"

Without pretense of waiting for agreement he began to set his astrogational and drive computers to take them on toward Hunters'. It would be another seventeen or eighteen standard days before *Orion* arrived in-system there. Exact timing was not possible in interstellar travel. It was something like piloting a sailing ship in a sea full of variable currents, depending upon winds that were undependable from day to day even though they held to a fairly consistent pattern. Variable stars, pulsars, spinars and quasars within the galaxy and out of it had each their effects upon the subfoundation of space through which the starship moved. Black holes of various sizes committed their wrenching gravitational enormities upon the fabric of the Universe. The explosions of supernovae far and near sent semi-eternal shock waves lapping at the hull. The interstellar ship that effectively outpaces light does not, cannot, carry aboard itself all the power needed to make it move as it does move. Only tapping the gravitational-inertial resources of the universe can provide such power, as the winds were tapped to drive the sailing ships of old.

Though the artificial gravity maintained its calm dominion in the lounge a change in lighting of the holographic chart signalled that *Orion* was underway. Schoenberg stood up, and stretched expansively, seeming to grow even bigger than he was. "On to Hunters'!" he announced. "Who'll join me in a drink? To the success of the hunt, and the enjoyment of any other amusements we may run into."

They all would have a drink. But Athena took only a sip before dropping her glass away into the recycling station. "Shall we get our chess tournament moving again, Oscar?"

"I think not." Schoenberg stood with one hand behind his back under the short tails of his lounging jacket, almost posing, savoring his own drink. "I'm going below. Time we got the firing range set up and got in a little practice. We're not going after pheasant, exactly . . . we'll have enough of tournaments after we land, perhaps." His intelligent eyes, lighted now by some private amusement, skipped around at all of them, seemed to linger longest, by a fraction of a second, on Suomi. Then Schoenberg turned and with a little wave went out of the lounge.

The party broke up. After taking his recorder back to his stateroom, Suomi started out again to see what the firing range was going to be like, and ran into De La Torre in the passageway.

Suomi asked: "What was that all about, 'enough of tournaments after we land'?"

"He's told you nothing about the tournament he wants to watch?"

"No. What kind?"

De La Torre smiled, and would not or could not give him a straight answer.

II

In the camp by the placid river, under Godsmountain's wooded flanks, there were sixty-four warriors when all were assembled at last, on this warm morning in the eastern-sunrise season. Out of the sixty-four there were not more than four or five who had ever seen each other before because they had come each from his own district, town, fiefdom, nomadic band or island, from every corner of the inhabitable world. Some had journeyed here from the shores of the boundless eastern ocean. Others had come from the edge of permanently inhabited territory to the north, where spring, already a sixtieth-of-an-old-man's-lifetime old, was melting free the glacier-beast and rime-worm. From the north came the mightiest hunters of this world named for hunting. Others of these warriors had come from the uncrossable shattered desert that lay to the west of the lands of men, and others still from the tangle of rivers and swamps in the south that blended finally into ocean again and blocked all travel in that direction.

The warriors who had gathered on this day for the beginning of Thorun's Tournament were

variously tall or short, lean or heavy, but only a
few were very young men, and none at all were
very old. All were notably violent men even on
this world of violence, but during the days of assembly they had camped here together in peace,
each on his arrival accepting without argument
whatever little plot of campground was assigned
him by Leros or one of the subordinate priests of
Thorun. In the center of the camp an image of
the god, dark-bearded and gold-diademed,
brooding with hand on sword-hilt, had been
erected on a field-altar, a small wooden plat-
form, and no warrior failed to place some offering before it. Some of the offerings were rich, for
some of the men who had come to fight in the
Tournament were wealthy.

However wealthy or powerful an entrant
might be, he came alone, unattended by any servants or well-wishers and carrying little more
than a heavy robe for shelter in addition to the
weapons of his preference. It was going to be a
holy tournament, regarded by the priests of
Thorun as so sacred that outside spectators were
barred—though there was scarcely a freeman on
the planet who did not yearn to watch. Nor were
outside servants needed. The assembled warriors and priests were to be served—luxuriously,
it appeared—by an almost equal number of
gray-clad male slaves whose dress marked them
as property of Godsmountain, of Thorun and his
servitors. No women were to be allowed within
the camp.

On this morning when the last warrior arrived, some slaves were making ready the flat

fighting arena of pounded earth, some ten paces in diameter. Other slaves prepared a midday meal and set aside offerings of fruit and meat for those who would wish to lay them on Thorun's altar. The smoke of the cooking fires rose into a sky that was quite clear and had something of the blueness of Earth's sky, and yet also something of yellowness and bitterness and brass.

From beyond the plumes of smoke the mountain looked down, an unfamiliar sight to almost all of those who had come here to fight. But it had been known since childhood in all their hearts and minds. On its top the priests of Thorun dwelt, and their god and his power with them, within the white walls of his sacred city. Women and animals and other prosaic necessities were up there too; slaves were taken up from time to time as needed to serve the dwellers but seldom or never did the slaves come down again; those at work this morning in the riparian meadow had all been imported for the occasion from tributary lands. Godsmountain's sizable armies never, except for select detachments, marched any nearer their own capital than the mountain's base. To most ordinary folk the summit and its citadel-city were unattainable.

Thorun himself dwelt there, and the demigod Mjollnir, his most faithful paladin. Other divinities visited from time to time: the gods of healing, justice, soil and weather, and growth and fecundity; and numerous demigods with ancillary responsibilities. But it was primarily Thorun's mountain, Thorun's religion, Thorun's world—except to those, generally restricted to the rim of the world these days, who did not like Thorun, or did not like the power wielded in his name by Godsmountain's priests. Hunters' was a planet of hunters and warriors, and Thorun was god of war and of the hunt.

A priest called Leros, of middle age, having seen three previous northern springs, and scarred by the violence of his youth, had been appointed by the High Priest Andreas to direct the Tournament. Leros was high in rank among the priests of Thorun, though not a member of the most secret Inner Circle. In his youth he had gained an almost legendary reputation as a fighter, and many of the best of these young heroes regarded him with awe. Leros came down to the riverbank himself to greet the last-arriving warrior, one Chapmut of Rillijax. He gave Chapmut a hand out of his canoe, bade him welcome to the Sacred Tournament of Thorun, and then with a small flourish placed the last checkmark on the tally sheet containing all the expected warriors' names.

Shortly after, a solemn drum called all of them to an assembly. Leros, standing in a new robe of spotless white in the center of the clean new arena, waited while they gathered around its edge. They were not long in falling silent to give him their full attention. In some parts of the circle the warriors were crowded, yet there was no jostling or edging for position among them, or anything but the greatest courtesy.

"Rejoice, ye chosen of the gods!" Leros cried out at last in his still-strong voice. He swept his gaze fully around the ring of fighting men, standing himself as tall and strong as most of them, though no longer as quick or sure. It was many days, about a sixtieth-part-of-an-old-man's-life, since the formal announcement of this Tournament had been carried down from Godsmountain and spread across the world. For much longer, since the time of the last northern spring, it had been common knowledge that this Tournament was coming. Scrawny little boys of that time were now men in their prime; and Godsmountain and all its doings had waxed greatly in importance since then.

Many of the waiting entrants were half naked in the mild weather, their bodies all muscles and scars and hair. The clothes of some were very rough, and those of others soft and rich. A few wore scraps of body armor, or carried shields of hardened sloth-leather or bright iron. Full armor was unknown on Hunters', where a man stood on his feet to fight and never rode. These fighters were chiefs' sons and peasants' sons and sons of unknown fathers. Nothing but merit, merit with sword and spear and battle-axe, had won them their places here. Around him now Leros saw blue eyes and dark eyes, eyes with epicanthic folds and eyes without, deep eyes here, mad eyes there, and a pair or two of eyes that seemed as innocent as babes'. The original colonists from Earth, some six standard centuries in the past, had been eclectically selected from a world already well mixed in race and culture. Around Leros the faces were brown or white or black, with hair of black or brown or yellow or red—

there was one iron-gray, two shaven bald. Here was a heavily tattooed face, with stripes across from ear to ear, and over there a smile showed teeth all filed to points. More numerous than the oddities were other men who looked as prosaic as herdsmen, save for the weapons at their belts. Besides their human maleness, only one thing was common to them all: uncommon skill at killing other men in single combat.

"Rejoice, ye chosen!" Leros called again, more softly. "Before the sun goes down upon this day, half of you will stand within our god's great hall—" he pointed toward Godsmountain's top, out of sight behind the wooded bulges of its lower slopes—"and face to face with Thorun himself." Leros prepared himself to retell, and his listeners made ready to hear yet again, the promises that had been carried down from Godsmountain a standard year earlier by Leros and his aides.

Thorun, warrior-chieftain of the gods (so the message went) had been pleased by the spirit shown by the race of men in the recent series of wars extending Godsmountain's power across most of the habitable world. The god was pleased to grant to humankind the privilege of fighting for a seat at his right hand, the competition being open to the sixty-four finest heroes of the age. To accomplish this purpose the inhabited world had been arbitrarily divided into sixty-four districts, and the local rulers of every district were invited to send—the details of the selection process being left largely to them—

their mightiest warrior. All but one of the contestants was expected to die in the Tournament of Thorun, and that one, the winner, would be granted the status of a demigod and would take his seat at Thorun's right hand. (Out in the country somewhere, some irreverent logician would be sure to ask the priest who brought the message: How about Mjollnir: Will he have to move down a peg? Not at all, my nephew. No doubt he and the Tournament winner will share the honor of being next to Thorun. No doubt they will fight for the day's turn whenever it pleases them.)

By all reports it pleased them to fight a lot in Thorun's hall atop the mountain. There the great god and the more or less deified men, slaughtered heroes of wars and combats past, re-slaughtered one another daily for the joy of it and were miraculously healed of their wounds each evening in time to enjoy the perfect meat and drink of Thorun's table, the tale-telling of immortal eloquence shared by the company of the gods, the endless supply of maidens eternally made virgin for their pleasure. (Out in the country, the questioner relaxes with a sigh; there is more here than a simple warrior knows how to argue about. Even if he is not so simple, the questioner sees that he is not going to beat this talking priest at his own game of words.)

Leros on this bright morning was formally spelling out once more what his listeners already knew: "Those of you who fall in the first round of fighting will be the first to feast with Thorun —but eternally around the lowest portion of his table. The next sixteen who perish, in the second round of fighting, will be granted places higher up. In the fighting of the third round eight will die and will be seated higher still—and each of these will have eternally with him four lovely maids of a beauty surpassing any in this world, two of ivory white and two of ebon black, to satisfy his every wish even before it can be spoken aloud.

"After the fourth round has been fought there will be only four warriors left alive, the strongest of the strong. The four who die in the fourth round of fighting will be granted shields and arms lustrous as silver, yet harder and keener than the finest steel, and wine goblets to match, and each will have eight virgin maidens of still greater beauty perpetually in his service. They will be seated very near to Thorun.

"In the fifth round of duels, two more men must fall, and these two will be seated in tall chairs of oak and gold, higher up the table still, and they will be granted gold winecups and shields and arms, and each will be served by sixteen maids of beauty indescribable, and all things will be theirs in fuller measure than any lower men may have. On that day but two of you will remain alive outside the hall where the gods feast.

"The single duel of the sixth round of fighting will be the last and greatest. Who loses it will still be honored beyond any of those that I have mentioned yet. And when it is over, the Tournament will be over, and one man will have won. That man alone shall walk, in the flesh, into the

holy place of the god Thorun, and his place for
all time to come shall be at Thorun's right hand;
and from his high place that man will overtop all
of the other sixty-three by as great a measure as
they stand above the race of puny, mortal men
that crawl about here below."

Leros concluded with a sigh. He believed the
promises and they moved him to envy and awe
every time he thought about them.

For some time now one of the warriors, black
of skin and huge, had been leaning forward with
an expectant look, as if he wished to speak. Now
Leros, with an inquiring glance, took notice of
him.

The man asked: "Lord Leros, tell me this—"

"Address me no more as Lord. Your status
from this day forward is higher than my own."

"Very well. Friend Leros, then. Tell me this:
when a man has won this Tournament will he
then have all the powers and rights that gods are
known to have? I mean not only powers of war,
but of the soft and healing arts?"

Leros had to take thought for a moment or
two before answering. It had not been one of the
usual expectable questions, for instance was
Thorun's hall threatened by overcrowding with
all the wars, or what kind of sacrificial meat
would the god prefer today. At last he spoke.
"The gentle goddess of healing will certainly listen to any request that man may make." He let
out a light sigh. "The gods listen to one another
more than they do to men. But then they still do
what they please, unless of course they have

bound themselves by formal promise, as Thorun has done regarding this Tournament."

The man nodded soberly. "It is all we can expect," he said, and resumed his place in the circle.

All were silent now. Somewhere in the background a slave was chopping kindling for the first funeral pyre. Leros said: "Then go, all of you, and make what final preparations you will. The first fight will begin shortly."

As soon as the assembly had dispersed a subordinate priest drew Leros aside and when they had reached a place of relative privacy unrolled a small scroll and showed it to him. "Lord Leros, this was found posted on a tree not far away. We have no clue as yet to indicate who put it up."

The lettering on the scroll seemed to have been made with a dull ordinary pencil of charred kettwood. The message read:

> Gods and men, place your bets. Who of the 64 will be proven the greatest fighter? That one will be, there is no doubt. Will he then envy those that he has slain, and curse Godsmountain and its lying priests? While your money is out, try to lay a bet on this also: Are the rulers of this mountain fit to rule our world?
>
>   The Brotherhood

Leros nodded, tight-lipped, at the signature. "You have sent word of this up the hill?"

"Of course, Lord."

"That is all we can do for the moment. We

must make sure the army increases its patrols in the area." But of course the message might have been put up by someone known to be in the area of the Tournament. Perhaps one of the slaves—or even one of the contestants—is not what he pretends to be. "We must keep our eyes open, of course, and let nothing jeopardize the Tournament. To discredit it would be a considerable victory for the Brotherhood." The Brotherhood was a vague league of the disaffected, probably including most of Godsmountain's enemies, who were now scattered and relatively powerless around the rim of the inhabited world. There might be a sharp and dangerous secret organization at its core; it seemed wise to assume there was, and to continually warn the people and the soldiers of it.

The subordinate indicated his agreement and withdrew. Leros pondered briefly: Might the agent who had left the message be a disloyal priest? He did not think it probable. But he could not be completely sure.

The Tournament meanwhile, had to get started. There had been no sign from up the hill that High Priest Andreas or any of his Inner Circle were coming down to watch. A pack train came into view on the lower reaches of the long road that wound its way down the forested slopes from the summit; but when it drew near Leros saw that no men of rank were walking near the animals, it was only a regular supply caravan returning unburdened from the top.

On with it, then. Turning to a waiting herald, he gave the signal for the battle-horn to be blown, to call the contestants all together for the last time in the world of living men. When they were assembled he drew from a pocket of his fine white robe a scroll of new vellum, on which a priest-scribe had set down the names in elegant calligraphy. They appeared in the alphabetical order hallowed by time and military usage:

Arthur of Chesspa
Ben Tarras of the Battle-Axe

Big Left Hand
Bram the Beardless of Consiglor

Brunn of Bourzoe
Byram of the Long Bridges

Chapmut of Rillijax
Charles the Upright

Chun He Ping the Strong
Col Renba

David the Wolf of Monga's Village
Efim Samdeviatoff

Farley of Eikosk
Farmer Minamoto

Geno Hammerhand
Geoff Symbolor of Symbolorville

Gib the Blacksmith
Giles the Treacherous of Endross Swamp

* * *

Gladwin Vanucci
Gunter Kamurata

Hal Coppersmith
Herc Stambler of Birchtown

Homer Garamond of Running Water
Ian Offally the Woodcutter

John Spokemaker of the Triple Fork
Jud Isaksson of Ardstoy Hill

Kanret Jon of Jonsplace
Korl the Legbreaker

LeNos of the Highlands
Losson Grish

M'Gamba Mim
Muni Podarces

Mesthles of the Windy Vale
Mool of Rexbahn

Nikos Darcy of the Long Plain
Oktans Buk of Pachuka

Omir Kelsumba
One-Eyed Manuel

Otis Kitamura
Pal Setoff of Whiteroads

Pern-Paul Hosimba
Pernsol Muledriver of Weff's Plain

Phil Cenchrias
Polydorus the Foul

Proclus Nan Ling
Rafael Sandoval

Rahim Sosias
Rico Kitticatchorn of Tiger's Lair

Rudolph Thadbury
Ruen Redaldo

Sensai Hagenderf
Shang Ti the Awesome

Siniuju of the Evergreen Slope
Tay Corbish Kandry

Thomas the Grabber
Thurlow Vultee of the High Crag

Travers Sandakan of Thieves' Road
Urumchi

Vann the Nomad
Venerable Ming the Butcher

Vladerlin Bain of Sanfa Town
Wat Franko of the Deep Wood

Wull Narvaez
Zell of Windchastee

When he had done with reading, Leros glanced up at the still-high sun. "There will be time today for much fighting. Let it begin."

He handed the scroll to a subordinate priest, who read in a loud voice: "Arthur of Chesspa— Ben Tarras of the Battle-Axe."

Having both stepped into the ring, and made their holy signs imploring Thorun's favor, the two went at it. Ben Tarras had taken only a dozen more breaths when his battle-axe spun out of his hand to bury itself with a soft sound in the calmly receiving earth, while Arthur's swordblade at the same time sank true and deep in Ben Tarras's flesh. The bare, flattened soil of the fighting ring drank Ben Tarras's blood as if it had been long athirst. A pair of slaves in shabby gray tunics dragged his body from the ring, toward a place nearby where other slaves were readying a pyre. The dry wood was stacked twice taller than a man already, and was not yet enough. Thirty-two men today would join the gods and begin their eternal feast with Thorun.

"Big Left Hand—Bram the Beardless of Consiglor."

This fight went on a little longer; and then both hands of Big Left Hand (they appeared equally big) were stilled as Bram's sword tore his middle open. Again the slaves came to bear a corpse away, but Big Left Hand stirred and

kicked feebly as they took him up. His eyes
opened and were living, though the terrible
wound in his front was plainly mortal. One
slave, who limped about his work, pulled from
his belt a short but massive leaden maul and
broke the head of the dying man with a short
methodical swing. Leros for the second time said
ritual words to speed a loser's soul to Thorun,
nodded to the acolyte who held the scroll.

"Brunn of Bourzoe—Byram of the Long
Bridges."

It went on through the afternoon, with little
pauses between fights. Some of the fights were
long, and one of the winners had lost so much
blood that he could hardly stand himself before
he managed to still the breath in the loser's
throat. As soon as each fight was over the slaves
came quickly to stanch the wounds, if any, of the
winner, and lead him to food and drink and rest.
It was likely to go hard in the second round of
fighting with those who had been weakened in
the first.

The sun was reddening near the horizon
before the last match had been fought. Before
retiring, Leros gave orders that the camp should
be moved early in the morning. Originally he
had planned to wait until midday before beginning the slow intended progress up the mountain, but the smoke of the funeral pyre seemed to
lie heavy here in the low air, and amphibious
vermin from the river were being drawn to the
camp by the blood of heroes in which the earth
was soaked.

III

Orion was well in-system now, rapidly matching orbital velocities with Hunters' planet, and in fact not far from entering atmosphere. From his command chair in the small control room at the center of the ship, Schoenberg supervised his autopilot with a computer-presented hologram of the planet drifting before him, the planet as it appeared in *gestalt* via the multitude of sensing instruments built into the starship's outer hull.

A few days earlier Suomi had obtained a printout on Hunters' planet from the ship's gazeteer, a standard databank carried for navigation, trade, and emergency survival. The Hunterian year was about fifteen times as long as the Earth-standard year; Hunters' planet was therefore much farther from its primary than Earth was from Sol, but Hunters' Star was a blue-white subgiant, so that the total insolation received by both planets was very nearly equal. The radius, mass, and gravity of Hunters' planet were Earthlike, as was the composition of the atmosphere. Hunters' would surely have been col-

onized from pole to pole had it not been for its
extreme axial tilt—more than eighty degrees to
the plane of its revolution around Hunters' sun,
almost as far as was Uranus in its orbit around
Sol.

Spring was now a standard year old in the
Hunterian northern hemisphere, which region
was therefore emerging from a night that had
been virtually total for another Earthly year or
so. Near the north pole the night had now lasted
for more than five standard years and would endure for a total of seven. Up there the ice-grip of
the dark cold was deep indeed, but it would soon
be loosened. Seven standard years of continuous
sunheat were coming.

According to statements in the gazeteer,
which were probably still valid though more
than a standard century old, men had never
managed to settle permanently much farther
than fifteen degrees of latitude in either direction
from the Hunterian equator. Dome colonies
would have been called for and there had never
been sufficient population pressure to make it
worthwhile. Indeed, the population had not occupied even the whole equatorial zone of the
main continent when the berserkers came. When
the killing machines from out of space attacked,
the growing technological civilization of
Hunters' colonists had been wrecked; the intervention of Karlsen's battle fleet was the only
reason that any of the colonists—or the
biosphere itself, for that matter—had survived at
all. The native life, though none of its forms were
intelligent, did manage to endure at all latitudes,

surviving the long winters by hibernation of one
kind or another, and in many cases getting
through the scorching, dessicated summers by
an estivation cycle.

Away from the tropics, spring presented the
only opportunity for feeding, growth, and reproduction. Because the southern hemisphere was
so largely water, the northern spring was the one
that counted insofar as land animals were concerned. In the northern springtime beasts of all
description emerged from caves and nests and
frozen burrows with the melting of the ice.
Among them came predators, more terrible,
burning with more urgent hunger and ferocity,
than any creatures that had ever lived on the old
wild lands of Earth. On Hunters' planet now, as
every fifteen standard years, the hunting season
by which the planet had acquired its name was
in full swing.

"The poaching season, I suppose we should
call it," said Carlos Suomi to Athena Poulson.
The two of them were standing in the shooting
gallery Schoenberg had set up a few weeks
earlier in the large cabin directly beneath *Orion*'s
lounge. Suomi and Athena were looking over a
large gun rack filled with energy rifles; Schoenberg had enjoined everyone aboard to select a
weapon and become adept with it before shooting in earnest was required. Schoenberg and De
La Torre spent a good deal of time down here,
Celeste and Barbara hardly any.

Suomi and Athena were intermediate, he generally showing up whenever she went to practice.

They were in mid-session now. Some ten meters
from the rifle rack—half the diameter of the
spherical ship—a computer-designed hologram
showed a handful of Hunterian predators stop-
actioned in what looked like a good drawing of
their natural habitat. Around and beyond the
sketch-like animals in the middle distance what
appeared to be several square kilometers of
glacier spread to an illusive horizon.

"All right," Athena said in her low voice.
"Technically speaking, this trip *is* outside interstellar law. But it's evident that neither the
authorities on Earth or the Interstellar Authority
care very much. Oscar is too smart to get into
any real trouble over such a thing. Relax and
enjoy the trip, Carl, now that you're here.
Whyever did you come along if you don't like the
idea?"

"You know why I came." Suomi pulled a rifle
halfway out of the rack and then slid it back. The
end of its muzzle was slightly bulbous, dull gray,
pitted all over with tiny and precisely machined
cavities. What it projected was sheer physical
force, abstracted almost to the point of turning
into mathematics. Suomi had already tried out
all the rifles in the rack and they all seemed pretty much the same to him, despite their considerable differences in length and shape and
weight. They were all loaded now with special
target cartridges, projecting only a trickle of
power when triggered, enough to operate the
target range. Its setup was not different in principle from the target ranges in arcades on Earth
or other urbanized planets; only there it was

generally toy berserkers that one shot at, black metal goblins of various angular shapes that waved their limbs or flashed their imitation laser beams in menace. "I've always enjoyed these target games," he said. "Why shouldn't these be real enough, instead of going after living animals?"

"Because these are not real," said Athena firmly. "And shooting at them isn't real either." She chose a rifle and turned her back on Suomi to aim it down the range. Somewhere a scanner interpreted her posture as that of the ready hunter, and the scene before her came alive again with deliberate motion. A multmouthed creature bristling with heavy fur stalked toward them at a range of seventy meters. Athena fired, a small click was emitted by the rifle, which remained perfectly steady, and the beast flopped over in a graceful, almost stylized way, now wearing a spot of red light riveted near the middle of what should have been its spine. The indication was for a clean kill.

"Athena, I came along because you were coming, and I wanted to spend time with you, to get some things settled between us. That's why I had you get me invited. Also it was a chance to take a trip on a private space yacht, something I'll probably never be able to do again. If I must hunt, to keep your lord and master upstairs happy, why then I'll do it. Or at least go through the motions of hunting."

"Carlos, you're always talking down Oscar to me, and it won't work. I think this is the one I'll carry." She turned the rifle this way and that, looking at it critically.

"I wonder what the people living on Hunters' think about expeditions like ours."

"They're not being harmed, as far as I can see. I don't suppose they'll give a damn, even if they know we're there, which they probably won't. We won't be hunting in an inhabited area, but in the north."

She sounded as if she knew what she was talking about, though she had probably only read the same ship's printout that Suomi had been studying. None of them except Schoenberg had been here before, and, when you thought about it, Schoenberg was really uncommunicative about his previous trip. With a few words he gave assurance that they were all in for some marvelous sport, warned succinctly about certain dangers to be wary of—and that was about it. He might have been on Hunters' a number of times before. He might be three hundred years old or more; it was getting hard to tell these days, when an age of five hundred years was not unheard of. As long as the central nervous system held out other systems of the body could generally be maintained or replaced as needed.

Schoenberg's voice now sounded on the intercom. "We're coming into atmosphere soon, people. Artificial gravity will be going off in another twenty minutes. Better secure your areas and settle in the lounge or in your staterooms."

"We hear you in the target range," Suomi answered. "We're on our way." He and Athena began to secure the rifles in the rack, and to make sure that nothing in the area was likely to

fly around loose if the coming maneuvers in free
gravity should become violent for any reason.

Seated a few minutes later in the lounge,
Suomi watched the progress of their descent on
the wall-sized screens. The planet, that had been
hardly more than a star when last he observed its
image, was now on top of them, or so it seemed.
It grew further, eased around to a position below
them as Schoenberg changed ship's attitude,
spread a cloud net to catch *Orion*, became a
world with a horizon to hold them in. The blue-
white sun grew yellowish as they began to see it
from inside the planet's atmosphere.

The land below was high, rough country. Like
most planets, Hunters' had an uninhabited look
when seen from the upper air. Here the appearance persisted even when they had dropped to
only a few kilometers' altitude.

Schoenberg, alone in the control room, now
took over control completely from the computers, guiding the ship manually, looking
rapidly from one television screen to another. In
the lounge they could watch him on the
passenger's screen. Obviously traffic in the
Hunterian atmosphere was practically non-exis-
tent and a mid-air collision nothing to be feared.

Now Schoenberg was following a river, actually skirting sometimes between the walls of its
deep-cut canyon. Mountains rose and dipped
beneath *Orion* as he veered away from the watercourse, steadily decreasing speed. At last a
chalet-like structure, flanked by log outbuild-
ings, the whole complex surrounded by a

palisade, came into view at the head of a pass.
There was a scarcity of level ground, but
Schoenberg had no real trouble in lowering the
ship onto the barren soil about fifty meters outside the stockade. From the spherical metal hull,
thick landing struts moved out to take the ship's
weight and hold her upright. There was a scarcely perceptible settling motion when the pilot cut
the drive. The ship used the same silent forces
for maneuvering in atmosphere as in space—
though caution was necessary when using them
near a planet-sized mass—and it could be
landed on any surface that would bear its
weight.

Obviously their descent had been observed,
for the drive was hardly off before people in drab
clothes began to appear from a gate in the stockade. The arrival of a spaceship seemed to be an
exciting event, but no more than that. The im-
promptu welcoming committee of six or eight
showed no hesitancy in drawing near.

Once the ship was firmly down Schoenberg
got out of his chair and headed for the main
hatch, which, without formality, he at once
opened wide to the planet's air, and pressed the
button to extrude a landing ramp. He and the
others aboard had taken the routine immunological treatments before departure, and
the ship had been gone over by his own medics
to avoid carrying dangerous microorganisms to a
planet with only a primitive medical technology.

The natives waited a few meters from the ship,
the women wearing long gowns and heavy
aprons, the men for the most part dressed in cov-

eralls. A couple of them had primitive cutting or digging tools in hand.

One smiling young man, better dressed than the others, his boots just as heavy but fancier, and with a short sword in a decorated leather scabbard at his belt, stepped forward.

"Welcome, then." He spoke the common language with what seemed to Earth ears a heavy, but understandable, accent. "Now you are Mister Schoenberg, I recall."

"I am." Smiling and open in his manner, Schoenberg went down the ramp to shake hands. "And you are—Kestand, isn't it? Mikenas's younger brother?"

"Now that is right. I was just a small one last hunting season when you were here. Surprised you know me."

"Not at all. How's Mikenas?"

"He's fine. Out now tending stock."

The conversation went on about the state of affairs on the ranch or fiefdom or whatever it was that the absent Mikenas owned or ruled. Suomi and the other passengers—all the girls were now dressed quite modestly—had come down from the lounge, but at a gesture from Schoenberg remained just inside the ship, enjoying the fresh alien air. Meanwhile the farm workers remained standing in a group outside. These all appeared cheerful and more or less healthy, but might have been deaf and dumb. It was probably a decade and a half since any of them had had any news from the great interstellar civilization that networked the sky about them. They smiled at the visitors, but only Kestand spoke, and even he showed no inclination to ask how things were going, out among the stars.

It seemed that no introductions were going to be made. The whole thing had a clandestine air, like a smugglers' meeting. For a moment Suomi wondered—but the idea was ridiculous. A man of Schoenberg's wealth would not dabble in smuggling so directly if he decided to take it up.

Kestand was asking: "Have you been hunting yet?"

"No. I wanted to stop here first, and find out what's changed on the world since my last trip."

"Well." Kestand, not the most scintillating speaker Suomi had ever attended, began to expand his earlier reports on the local state of crops and weather and hunting. "Not real northern hunting, y'understand, I haven't been able to get away yet this season. Like to be on my way right now, but Mikenas left me in charge."

Schoenberg was listening patiently. Suomi, from clues dropped here and there, gathered that Mikenas and Schoenberg had gone north by spaceship last hunting season and had enjoyed notable success. Suomi's eyes kept coming back to the sword Kestand wore. The sheath was leather, looped onto the man's belt, and the hilt seemed to be plastic but of course was much more likely to be wood or bone; Suomi wished he knew more about primitive materials. Casting back through his life's memories—only about thirty years to be sure—he could not recall ever before seeing a man carrying a weapon for any non-symbolic purpose. Of course this sword might be only a badge of authority. It looked, though, as business-like as the hoe that one of the other men was holding.

The two-way conversation had veered to the governmental and religious changes that had taken place since the last northern hunting season. These were all obscure to Suomi, but Schoenberg seemed to understand.

"Godsmountain has pretty well taken over, then," he mused, nodding his head as if at a suspicion confirmed. Then he asked: "Are they having the Tournament as planned this season?"

"Yes." Kestand looked up at the sun. "Should be starting in another two, three days. Byram of the Long Bridges, he's our local champion."

"Local?" Schoenberg looked thoughtful. "Isn't Long Bridges a good two hundred kilometers from here?"

"I tell you, this's a world Tournament. Each of the sixty-four districts is a big'un." Kestand shook his head. "I'd purely like to go."

"You would've gone, I bet, even rather than hunting, if Mikenas hadn't left you in charge here."

"No, oh nooo, there was no way. Tournament's private for the gods and priests. Even the earl couldn't get an invitation, and Byram is his bodyguard. Mikenas didn't even try."

Schoenberg frowned slightly, but did not pursue the matter of the Tournament any further. Suomi meanwhile was imagining a tour-

nament of jousting, as in the old stories of Earth,
men in full armor hurtling together on armored
animals, trying to unseat each other with lances.
But it couldn't be quite that; he recalled from his
reading that there were no riding animals on
Hunters'.

After a little more talk Schoenberg thanked
his informant courteously and called up into the
ship for them to hand him down a satchel from
a locker near the hatch. "And two of those ingots
that you'll find in the locker; bring them down
also, would you, gentlemen?"

Suomi and De La Torre brought the desired
items down the ramp. Setting the satchel at
Kestand's feet, Schoenberg announced: "This is
what I told Mikenas I'd bring him, power cells
for lamps and a few medicines. Tell him I'm
sorry I missed him; I'll stop again next season if
all goes well. And here." He hefted the two ingots and handed them to the native. "For you.
Good metal for points or blades. Have a good
smith work it. Tell him to quench it in ice water.
I guess you have no trouble getting that at this
altitude."

"Why, I give you great thanks!" Kestand was
obviously well pleased.

Once the ramp was retracted and the hatch
closed, Schoenberg wasted little time in getting
Orion into the air again. He still held manual
control, soaring up in a steep arc that gradually
bent into a level flight toward the northwest.

His passengers had come to the control room
with him this time and sat or stood around, more
or less looking over his shoulder. When they had

leveled off, De La Torre asked: "Where to, fearless leader? Shall we go and watch a few heads get broken?"

Schoenberg grunted. "Let's go hunting first, Gus. The man said two or three days before the Tournament starts. I'm anxious to get a little hunting in." This time he remembered to look around as a matter of form. "How does that suit you people?"

The planet flowed south and east beneath them. The sun, turning blue-white again at this altitude, reversed its apparent daily motion proper for the season and also slid toward the east from the tearing high-Mach velocity of their flight. An indicator on the edge of a warning zone showed how the drive was laboring to move them at so high a velocity this close to the center of a planet-sized mass. Schoenberg was indeed impatient. He had run out force-baffles on the hull, Suomi noted, to dampen the sonic shock wave of their passage, and they were too high to be seen from the ground with unaided eyes. No one in the lands below would be able to detect their passage.

Celeste and Barbara soon retired to re-decorate themselves in interstellar style. For the next several days the party would presumably be out of sight of Hunterian males who might be aroused or scandalized by the fashions of the great world.

Athena, clinging to a stanchion behind Schoenberg's chair, remarked: "I wonder if there are other hunting parties here. Out-worlders like us, I mean."

Schoenberg only shrugged. Suomi said: "I
suppose there might be three or four. Not many
can afford private space travel, and also have the
inclination to hunt."

De La Torre: "Since we all seem to have the
inclination to hunt, it's lucky for us that we
found Oscar."

Oscar had no comment. Suomi asked De La
Torre: "Do you work for him, by the way?
You've never told me."

"I have independent means, as they say. We
met through business, about a year ago."

Schoenberg had gone a little higher to ease the
strain on the drive. At this altitude the world
called Hunters' almost seemed to have let go of
the ship again. On several of the wall screens the
terminator, boundary line between night and
day, could be seen slanting across cloud cover
athwart the invisible equator far to the south.
The south pole, well out of sight around the
curvature of the world, was more than halfway
through its approximately seven standard years
of uninterrupted sunlight. There the sun was a
standard year past its closest approach to the ze-
nith, and was now spiralling lower and ever lower in the sky, one turn with every Hunterian day,
or one about every twenty standard hours.

A couple of standard years in the future the
sun would set for its long night at the south pole
and simultaneously rise above the horizon at the
north pole. Right now the Hunterian arctic,
locked in the last half of its long night, must look
as lifeless as the surface of Pluto, buried under a
vast freeze-out of a substantial portion of the

planet's water. Up there the equinoctial dawn
would bring the hunting season to its end; right
now the season was at its height in the middle
latitudes of the north, where the sun was just
coming over the horizon, each day sweeping
from east to west a little higher in the southern
sky, bringing in the thaw. That region must be
Schoenberg's destination.

They came down into a world of icy twilight,
amid slopes of bare enduring rock and eroding,
fantastic glaciers, all towering above valleys
filled with rushing water and greenly exploding
life.

Schoenberg found a walkable part of the landscape in which to set *Orion* down and some solid
level rock to bear her weight. This time, before
opening the hatch, he took a rifle from the small
rack set just inside, and held it ready in his
hands. The opening of the hatch admitted a
steady polyphonic roar of rushing waters.
Schoenberg drew a deep breath and stood in the
opening, looking out. As on the earlier landing
the others were behind him. Celeste and
Barbara, not dressed for near-freezing weather,
moved shivering to the rear. The air smelled of
wetness and cold, of thawing time and alien life.
The landscape stretched before them, too big
and complex to be quickly taken in. The shadows of southern mountains reached up high on
the mountains to the north.

They were going out right away; there were several standard hours of daylight remaining here.
Schoenberg began a routine check-out of arms and

other equipment, and called for volunteers.

Athena announced at once that she was ready.
De La Torre said that he would like to have a go.
Suomi, too—not that he really intended to kill
anything that did not attack him. He felt a genu-
ine need to get out of the ship for a while.
Though all the tricks of environmental psychology had been used in the interior design of the
Orion to ameliorate the reality of confinement,
the trip had still cooped up six people in a small
space for many weeks. Being aware of all the
designer's tricks, Suomi was perhaps helped less
than others by them. Barbara and Celeste
elected not to try hunting today after Schoenberg had indicated he preferred it that way. He
promised them a more peaceful picnic outing in
the morning.

"We'll go in pairs, then," Schoenberg announced when everything was ready. "Gus,
you've hunted before, but not on this planet. If I
may suggest, you and Athena take a stroll down
the valley there." It spread before them as they
looked out from the hatch, beginning thirty or
forty meters from the rocky level where the ship
rested, plunging after about a kilometer and a
half of gentle, green-clad slope into an ice-
clogged canyon down whose center a new tor-
rent had begun to carve its way. "Down there at
the lower end, where it slopes off into the canyon, the vegetation may well be head-high.
There should be twelve or thirteen species of
large herbivores."

"In that little space?" De La Torre interrupted.

"In that little space." Now that he was going
hunting, Schoenberg sounded more relaxed and
happy than at any time on the trip before. "Life
doesn't just thaw out here in the spring—it ex-
plodes. There'll be large predators in that valley
too, or I miss my guess. You don't want to run
into one an arm's length away, so better skirt the
taller growth. Carlos and I are going to take the
upper path." This climbed a rocky slope on the
other side of the ship. Suomi, during their descent, had glimpsed higher meadows in that direction. "We may find something really hungry
up there, just out of a high cave and on its way
down into the valleys for its first meal in a year
or two."

Boots, warm clothing, weapons, communicators, a few emergency items—all in order. Suomi was the last to get down the ramp
and crunch his new boots on Hunterian soil.
Almost before his feet were off the ramp it began
to fold up and retract. If the playgirls stayed inside with the hatch closed they would be perfectly safe until the men returned.

Athena and Gus waved and set off on the lower way, tendrils of grass-like groundcover whip-
ping about their boots. "Lead on up the path,"
said Schoenberg, with an uphill gesture to
Suomi. "I'm sure your nerves are okay—just a
matter of principle that I don't like a novice
hunter with a loaded firearm walking behind
me, when something to shoot at may jump out
ahead." The voice was charming if the words
were not, and they were said with a happy and
friendly look. All was right with Schoenberg at

the moment, obviously; he was eager to get going.

There was not really a path to follow, of course, but Suomi moved on up the spine of hill that formed the natural route Schoenberg must have meant to indicate.

Suomi as he climbed was soon lost in admiration of the country around him. Wherever the melting away of the winter's ice had left a few square centimeters of soil exposed, rank vegetation had sprung up. There were no tree-sized plants in evidence, nothing that seemed to have begun to grow more than a few days or weeks ago. In most places the grass- and vine-like things were no more than waist high, but frequently they grew so thickly that no glimpse of soil could be seen between the stems. The plants were striving madly, ruthlessly, for water and warmth and sunlight, leaping into growth, making what they could of the wet season before the long searing drought of summer began.

He paused, coming in sight of a meadow where man-sized creatures like giant slugs were moving, voraciously feeding on the plants, the wrinkles visibly stretching out of their grayish, hairless bodies.

"Rime-worms," said Schoenberg, who came up close behind him and disregarded the creatures after the first glance. "Look sharp now, there may be something after them."

"Do any of the larger forms freeze solidly through the night?"

"Biologists I've talked to say it's not possible.

But I don't think anyone knows for sure." Now that they had stopped, Schoenberg was studying the country with binoculars. They had put a little rocky bulge of hill between themselves and the spaceship, and were now out of sight and sound of anything manmade save what they carried with them. The tracks they had left behind them in occasional patches of slush or muddy turf were the only signs of past human activity. The world around them had been made virgin by death and resurrection.

Suomi was studying the country too, but not with binoculars and not for game. The yellowed sun was skimming a low point in the mountainous horizon, and seemed on the point of setting; actually there must still be an hour or so of daylight left. On the other side of a wide valley a glacier groaned, shed a few tons of cornice, broke out with a clear new waterfall. The organ-notes of older cataracts held steady in the distance. Gradually, as Suomi began to comprehend the scene fully, as he got beyond the stage of simple elation at getting outdoors again, he realized that he had never before beheld a scene of nature so beautiful and awesome, nothing that even came close. Not even the wonders and terrors of space, which, when they could be perceived at all, were beyond the scale and grasp of human appreciation. This thundering world of mountains and valleys, with its exploding life, was not beyond the human scale, not quite.

Schoenberg was less content with what he saw. Of predators he had evidently discovered no sign. "Let's move on a little," he said tersely,

putting his binoculars away. Suomi led on
again. When they had gone a few hundred
meters more, Schoenberg called another halt,
this time at the foot of a steep slope.

After another short session with the
binoculars, Schoenberg pointed up the hill and
said: "I'm going up there and have a look
around. Let me do this alone, I want to be quiet
and inconspicuous about it. Stay here, don't
move around, keep your eyes open. There may
be something on our trail, stalking us, and you
may get a good shot just by waiting."

With a faint thrill of danger, small enough to
be enjoyable, Suomi looked back along the way
they had come. Nothing moved but the distant,
harmless rime-worms. "All right."

He sat down and watched Schoenberg up the
slope and out of sight over the top of it. He then
swiveled around on his rocky seat, enjoying the
absence of people in every direction. It was de-
lightful to be alone, for the first time in—it
seemed like the first time in his life. Isolation
could be accomplished in the ship, of course, but
the others' bodies and minds were always there,
one was always aware of them only a few meters
away. Suomi touched the communicator on his
belt. The channels among hunters and between
the hunters and the ship were alive but so far
totally unused. Everyone was enjoying the physical and psychic separation.

Time passed. Schoenberg was gone longer
than Suomi had expected. A thin shadow came
over the nearby scenery as the sun declined behind a distant rim of ice: Without preamble a

magnificent glacier-beast appeared before
Suomi's eyes, perhaps two hundred fifty meters
off, across a gentle slope of detritus fallen from
an extension of the slope at the foot of which
Suomi waited. It was not the direction from
which Schoenberg had thought a predator was
likely to come, nor was the creature looking toward Suomi. It was facing downhill, turning its
head back and forth. Suomi raised his
binoculars, and recalled his reading. An excellent specimen, male, probably second-cycle,
just awakened from the second hibernation of its
life into its full prime of strength and ferocity.
The hollowness of loins and ribs was visible despite the thickness of orange-yellow fur. It was
rather larger than an Earthly tiger.

Suomi, without getting to his feet, raised his
rifle in perfectly steady hands and aimed. He
was only playing. He lowered the weapon again.

"Long shot for a beginner," said Schoenberg's
voice from close behind him, a little way up the
slope. The cataract-roar must swallow the voice
before the beast could hear it, even as it had kept
Suomi from hearing Schoenberg's approach
among the rocks. "But a clean one. If you don't
want to try it I'll have a crack."

Suomi knew without turning that Schoenberg
would already be raising his rifle to take aim.
Still without looking around, Suomi lifted his
own weapon once more and fired (pop, a little
louder than in the shooting gallery, and now at
full power there was a perceptible kick), deliberately aiming ahead of the animal to frighten
it away, blasting up a spray of ice. Catlike, the

creature crouched, then turned toward the
earthmen its aliently unreadable face. The men
who lived on Hunters' were men of Earth in their
ancestry and distant history; it was easy to forget
how alien all the other life-forms here must be.

Now the glacier-beast was running, crossing
the slope in great graceful catlike bounds. But it
was not fleeing from the men as it should, as
Suomi had unthinkingly assumed it must. In
pure innocence of the powers it faced it was coming now to kill and eat him. Insane hunger drove
it on. Its sprinting taloned feet hurled up rocks
from the talus slope, mixed with a powdering of
snow.

Shoot. Whether Schoenberg was calling out the
word, or he himself, or whether it only hung
thought-projected in the freezing, timeless air,
Suomi did not know. He knew only that death
was coming for him, visible, and incarnate, and
his hands were good for nothing but dealing out
symbols, manipulating writing instruments,
paintbrushes, electronic styluses, making an impression on the world at second or third remove,
and his muscles were paralyzed now and he was
going to die. He could not move against the
mindless certainty he saw in the animal's eyes,
the certainty that he was meat.

Schoenberg's rifle sounded, a repetitive, seemingly ineffectual popping not far from Suomi's
right ear. Invisible fists of god-like power
slammed at the charging animal, met the beautiful energy of its charge with a greater, more
brutal force. The force-blows tore out gobs of

orange-yellow fur, and distorted the shapes of
muscle and bone beneath. The huge body shed
its grace and its momentum. Still it seemed to be
trying to reach the men. Now its body broke
open along a line of penetration wounds, spilling
out insides like some red-stuffed toy. Clear in
Suomi's vision was an open paw with knife-long
claws, arching high on the end of a forelimb and
then striking down into a puddle of slush not ten
meters from his boots.

When the beast was still, Schoenberg put another shot carefully into the back of its head for
good measure, then slung his rifle and got out his
hologram camera. Then, after looking at the
gory, broken body from several angles, he shook
his head and put the camera away again. He
spoke reassuringly to Suomi, seeming not in the
least surprised or upset by Suomi's behavior. He
was offhandedly gracious when Suomi at last
managed to stammer out a kind of thanks. And
that in its way was the most contemptuous attitude that Schoenberg could have taken.

IV

Early on the morning of the Tournament's
second day, Leros, the priest in charge, led the
surviving thirty-two contestants on an easy
march of some five kilometers, up from the flat
land by the river where the first round had been
fought to a much higher meadow resting in
Godsmountain's lap. At this new site an advance
party of priests and workers were already at
work, preparing a new fighting ring of cleared,
hard-trodden earth, and a new field altar for the
image of Thorun that was brought up on a cart
just in front of Leros and the warriors. The slave-
laborers were sweating, earning their rations today, for their numbers had been greatly reduced,
many being sent to other projects. Only half the
original number of warriors now required service, of course, and as always there was plenty of
other labor to be performed in the citadel-city
above and the tributary lands below.

The plan of the Tournament, handed down to
Leros by the High Priest Andreas and his Inner
Circle of councillors, required that each suc-
cessive round of fighting take place closer to the

53

top of the mountain than the one before. The
purpose, as Andreas had explained it, was symbolic. But Leros observed now that the plan had
practical advantages as well. The offal of each
camp would be promptly left behind, the latrine,
the leavings of the cook-tents, the remnants of
the funeral pyre.

The work of readying the new site was completed shortly after the fighting men arrived, and
an acolyte handed over the day's new vellum-
written lists to Leros. He called the men into assembly, and, when some formalities had been
gotten out of the way, read the lists out:

Arthur of Chesspa
Bram the Beardless of Consiglor

Brunn of Bourzoe
Charles the Upright

Col Renba
Efim Samdeviatoff

Farley of Eikosk
Geoff Symbolor of Symbolorville

Giles the Treacherous of Endross Swamp
Gladwin Vanucci

Hal Coppersmith
Homer Garamond of Running Water

Jud Isaksson of Ardstoy Hill
Kanret Jon of Jonsplace

LeNos of the Highlands
M'Gamba Mim

Mesthles of the Windy Vale
Octans Bukk of Pachuka

Omir Kelsumba
Otis Kitamura

Pernsol Muledriver of Weff's Plain
Polydorus the Foul

Rafael Sandoval
Rahim Sosias

Rudolph Thadbury
Shang Ti the Awesome

Siniuju of the Evergreen Slope
Thomas the Grabber

Travers Sandakan of Thieves' Road
Vann the Nomad

Vladerlin Bain of Sanfa Town
Wull Narvaez

Before giving the signal for the start of the second round's first fight, Leros took a moment to look around him at his world. There was much in it to make him feel content. From the high meadow where he stood the prospect was one of long reaches of cultivated land below, kilometer

after kilometer of field and pasture, with here
and there an orchard, a cluster of houses, a
patch of raw forest or a string of trees along a
watercourse. It was a peaceful and malleable
world, one of peasants and crops and artisans,
obediently serving the master of violence who
dwelt on the heights above. There was, of course,
the Brotherhood to flaw it. After yesterday's
posted insult nothing further had been heard
from them . . . there was also, more naggingly,
the fact that the Inner Circle seemed to be closed
to Leros, and the office of High Priest, therefore,
forever unattainable. Why should a priest like
Lachaise, for example, who was far more an
artisan than a fighting man, be a member of the
Inner Circle, when Leros and others more de-
serving were kept out?

At any rate the Tournament was going well.
That was what mattered most. Perhaps if it was
a great success he would at last be promoted—
and there was no reason why it should not
smoothly run its course. At the end of it the great
gate of the city would open for the winner as the
maidens strewed flowers before him and he was
conducted in triumph through the streets to the
Temple; and that would stand open for him
also; and then the inner curtains of chain-mail
would part—as they never had for Leros—and
the secret doors, and the winner would be let in
where Leros himself had never been to the place
where gods walked with the fallen heroes who
once were mortal men, where only the High
Priest and the Inner Circle came to mediate between them and the world of men.

* * *

Leros's religion was not simply a matter of faith to him. He had once glimpsed Thorun in an inner courtyard of the Temple, standing taller than any mortal man, walking with the High Priest on a night when storms were in the air and lightning flickered . . .

He bowed his head for a moment of private prayer, then brought himself back to the waiting men, and his responsibilities, and called out the names for the first match of the day:

"Arthur of Chesspa—Bram the Beardless of Consiglor."

Arthur was a middle-aged man of middle size. In this company of warriors he looked small. Stocky, dour-looking, heavily mustached, he strode into the ring with an air of utterly nerveless competence and with unblinking calm watched Bram the Beardless approach with intent to kill.

Bram, it appeared, was beardless by reason of his extreme youth. Though he was tall and heavy-shouldered his face looked no more than one Hunterian year of age, fifteen or sixteen sixtieths-of-an-old-man's-life. Bram was not calm but his excitement seemed to be rather joy than fright as he opened the attack with an exuberant swing of his long sword. Arthur parried the blow well enough, seemed in no hurry to go on the offensive himself.

Bram pressed the attack; his youth and energy did not admit the possibility that he could be beaten. Again and again he struck, while Arthur still retreated thoughtfully, seeming to await the

perfect time to counter. And again and again
Bram struck, with ever-increasing speed and terrible strength. Arthur still had not made up his
mind how best to fight when there came a blow
he could not stop. He lost an arm and shoulder.
The finishing stroke came quickly.

"Brunn of Bourzoe—Charles the Upright."

Brunn was heavyset and fair, with a sun-
bleached look about him. In one thick hand he
held a short spear in such fashion that it was
evident he preferred to thrust rather than risk all
on one throw. He took the initiative, though
cautiously, moving slowly widdershins around
the upright Charles. Charles gangly as a bird,
looking as if he might be happier perching on
one leg, stood tall and held his two-handed
sword ready for whatever Brunn might do. The
spear-thrust, when it came, was strong and
quick but the response of Charles was better; the
lopped-off spearhead fell to earth. The fair head
of Brunn was not far behind it.

"Col Renba—Efim Samdeviatoff."

These two were similar in appearance, both a
little above middle height and with brown
shaggy hair. Col Renba whirled a spike-studded
ball on the end of a short chain attached to a
wooden handle. Samdeviatoff held sword and
dagger ready. Both jumped to the attack at the
same time but the spiked ball struck the sword
out of the hand that held it and in the next
breath dashed the brains that had directed it
upon the ground.

"Farley of Eikosk—Geoff Symbolor."

Again there was a resemblance; this time one

of manners rather than appearance. Both contestants were well dressed and expensively
armed. There were even jewels in the hilts of
Geoff's sword and dagger. Farley was fair,
almost red, of hair and beard. His bare arms,
lined with bone and vein and muscle, were
freckled rather than sunburned. Geoff Symbolor
was quite dark, and shorter than Farley by half
a head, though seemingly his equal in weight
and strength. Their battle was a slow one. The
two of them seemed well matched until Farley's
longer reach let him nick the muscles of Geoff's
shoulder. With his sword-arm handicapped the
shorter man was soon wounded again. Farley
took no rash chances; the other was weakened
by loss of blood before Farley drove in hard to
finish him.

"Giles the Treacherous—Gladwin Vanucci."

Giles was of middling size but wiry, with
tanned face and sandy hair and pale innocent
eyes. If it was indeed his habit to be treacherous,
there was no need for it today. With his long
sword he made short work of the squat and
massive Gladwin, who had favored a battle-axe.

"Hal Coppersmith—Homer Garamond."

Hal Coppersmith was very tall, with sloping
shoulders and long arms entwined by rich
tattoos. His long sword quivered restlessly in his
hand, like some insect's antenna following the
movements of his foe. Homer Garamond seemed
saddened by the task at hand though he was
almost as young as Bram the Beardless who had
shone with joy in killing. Homer held sword and
dagger almost negligently in powerful hands un-

til Hal came thrusting in. Fast as Homer moved
then it was not fast enough.

"Jud Isaksson—Kanret Jon."

Jud, a fiery little man with an enormously
long black mustache, stamped briskly into the
ring with a round metal shield strapped onto his
left arm. A short sword extended from his right.
Kanret, perhaps the oldest fighter to survive the
first round, awaited him with a patience befit-
ting his years. Kanret was armed with a short,
thick-shafted spear; the way he gripped it indicated he might use it as a quarterstaff as well
as thrust with it. When the moment of testing
came, the spear hit nothing but Jud's shield, and
Kanret Jon was brought down with a
swordstroke to the knee. His end was quick
thereafter.

"LeNos of the Highlands—M'Gamba Mim."

LeNos had a scarred face and, once in the
ring, a way of moving that seemed more animal
than human, a lithe long-striding crouch. With
sword and dagger he closed on M'Gamba Mim,
who was huge and black and carried similar
weapons. The blood of both was on the ground
before LeNos could prevail; and then, still like
an animal, he snarled at the slaves who came to
tend his cuts.

"Mesthles of the Windy Vale—Octans Bukk
of Pachuka."

Mesthles had the thought-creased forehead of
some scribe or scholar. He wore peasant's
clothes and fought with a farmer's scythe. Octans was lean, and his ragged clothes gave him
the look of a hungry bandit. But his sword

proved slower than the scythe and he was mown.

"Omir Kelsumba—Otis Kitamura."

Kelsumba's wide black face was set in a determination as intense as fury. Leros, watching, remembered this man as the one who had asked about acquiring the healing powers of a god. When the fighters closed, Kelsumba swung his massive battle-axe with incredible power, swinging and then reversing instantly for the backswing—as if his weapon were no heavier than a stick. Kitamura's sword was knocked aside, and then Kitamura's jawbone. He went down on hands and knees and stayed there. Kelsumba left his finishing to the leaden mauls of the burial party.

"Pernsol Muledriver—Polydorus the Foul."

The Muledriver was an older man, who set to work deliberately with short spear and long knife. Polydorus, a man of indeterminate age, and seemingly no fouler than the next, went in carrying an old sword, much nicked and dented. The old sword did its work efficiently, and Pernsol died quietly, as if content to end life's struggles and take his modest place at Thorun's board.

"Rafael Sandoval—Rahim Sosias."

Sosias looked more like a tailor than a fighting man, being not overly big and displaying a small, comfortable paunch. But his curved sword hung as naturally from his hand as his hand from the end of his hairy arm. Sandoval was notably ugly, made so by nature, not by scars. He twirled a spike-and-ball mace disdainfully. Rahim's sword was caught in a loop of the mace's chain and pulled from his hand, but before Rafael could disentangle his own weapon from the sword, Rahim had drawn an extra knife from concealment and had slit his opponent's throat.

"Rudolph Thadbury—Shang Ti the Awesome."

Thadbury had a military as well as a fighting look. Leros thought this man had something more of the general than of the simple swordsman about him but knew nothing of his background. Most of the contestants were as much strangers to Leros and the other priests as they were to one another.

Squarely built, with blunt-fingered enormous hands, Rudolph Thadbury exuded strength and confidence. Shang Ti was awesome in truth, having a rather small head set on such a giant's body that the head's smallness was made to look grotesque. Shang Ti's sword was of a size to suit his stature. Rudolph's had a thicker blade than the usual and was just long enough to reach Shang Ti's heart.

"Siniuju of the Evergreen Slope—Thomas the Grabber."

Siniuju was almost scrawny, leaner than any other man left alive among the warriors. He carried a two-handed sword that looked too heavy for him—until he demonstrated how quickly he could make it move. Thomas was large and fierce-looking, a Shang Ti slightly less massive and better proportioned. He matched his spear over the long two-handed sword. The spear proved longer still.

"Travers Sandakan—Vann the Nomad."

Sandakan came carrying a thin-bladed axe made with a sturdy armored shaft. On his face were the lines of time and trouble and the scars of many fights. Vann the Nomad wore the long shapeless sweater of the high-plains herdsmen and wielded a long sword with demonic energy. Sandakan was no match for the Nomad and when Travers was dead Vann cut off one of his ears, saying: "I will give this back to him in Thorun's hall—if he is man enough to take it from me!" It was a gesture new to Leros, who thought about it and finally gave a hesitant smile of approval. As soon as the latest corpse had been cleared from the ring he formally called out the names for the day's final match.

"Vladerlin Bain—Wull Narvaez."

Coiled around Bain's waist was a long whip, whose purpose none had yet considered it politic to ask. In his hands Bain wore a dagger and a sword. Narvaez, with a cheerful foolish face and a farmer's pitchfork as his only visible weapon, looked like some peasant fresh from fieldwork. A good harvester he sent the tines exactly where he wanted them and Vladerlin was dead before he hit the ground, the reason for his coiled whip now never to be known.

The sun had not yet reached its midday point. The fighting of the second round was over.

The sixteen fighters who remained alive moved off to enjoy the food prepared for them. For the most part they chatted and joked in good fellowship, though a few were silent. Also they took thoughtful notice of each other's wounds, calculating where weakness would be found tomorrow. All of them knew that even the tiniest advantage must be seized. Not one survived among them who was not extremely dangerous —not one survived who could not count killers of superior ability among his victims.

Resting after their midday meal, they say the messenger come pelting down the mountain. His news made Leros snap back his head to search the sky. From where they camped beneath the trees it was not possible to see much of it. The warriors were curious, but not very. The Tournament they were engaged in was more important than any distraction they could imagine.

Later still when a priest of the Inner Circle came down to talk earnestly to Leros the news spread among the warriors that a round, silvery craft had come from beyond the world to visit Godsmountain. Most of them were curious enough to try to catch a glimpse of the ship, barely visible, resting among the trees on a distant height.

V

Oscar Schoenberg and Athena Poulson and
Gus De La Torre had hunted again, on the day
after Suomi's near-fatal confrontation with the
glacier-beast, while Barbara Hurtado and
Celeste Servetus had gone through the motions
of hunting. Suomi had chosen to stay with the
ship. Oscar and Athena and Gus, all having had
some excitement on their first day's hunt but
having returned from it empty handed returned
from the second day's effort with their hologram
trophies of large predators, safely recorded on
little crystal cubes for later reproduction and display.

Athena, sitting in the lounge, rubbing her
tired feet, complained it was going to be difficult
to find a place to show off her glacier-beast. "It's
all right for you, scar, but I have one small apartment. I'll have to move half the furniture to make
all right for you, Oscar, but I have one small
apartment. I'll have to move half the furniture to
make room for this—if I dare display it at all,
that is."

"Because you got it on an off-limits hunting trip?" Schoenberg laughed. "If anybody bothers you, just tell 'em I gave it to you. Let 'em come see me."

"I'll have to leave it turned off most of the time, just bring it out for special occasions. I suppose it would scare off most of my usual visitors, anyway." Then she caught herself and started to look apologetically toward Suomi, then hastily looked away.

Yesterday after everyone had returned to the ship they had all listened with some embarrassment to his account of how he had frozen in panic in the field and how Schoenberg had coolly saved his life. Athena had been more embarrassed, perhaps, than Suomi. De La Torre had seemed inwardly amused, and Barbara had shown some sympathy.

Suomi wondered if his shipmates—Athena especially—were waiting for him to demand a rifle and a chance to go out and prove himself. If so they were going to have a long wait. All right, he had been terrified. Maybe if he went out again and an animal charged, he wouldn't be terrified. Or maybe he would. He wasn't anxious to find out. He had nothing to prove. While all the others were out hunting on the second day he sat on the ship's extended landing ramp enjoying the air. There was a rifle at hand for emergencies but if anything menacing came in sight he planned to simply go inside and close the hatch.

Once everyone who wanted a trophy had one Schoenberg dallied in the north no longer. The

hunting season would last a long time but the
mysterious Tournament was apparently quite
brief and he didn't want to miss it. When Suomi
mentioned the Tournament to the girls, none of
them had any clear idea of what it was. Some
sort of physical contest, he supposed.

Schoenberg evidently knew the way to Godsmountain, though he said he had not been there
before. Flying south, he went much slower and
lower than on the northward flight, paying close
attention to landmarks. He followed a river valley most of the way, first by radar because of
ground fog, then visually when the view had
cleared. When, after several hours, they reached
their destination, there was no mistaking it.
Godsmountain stood out immediately from its
surroundings, a wooded eminence practically
isolated amid a patchwork of surrounding flat
farmlands, orchards and pastures. The mountain was broad and quite high, but in general not
very steep. On the deforested summit a town-
sized complex of white stone walls and buildings
stood out as plainly as if it had been constructed
as a beacon for aerial navigation.

After circling the mountain once at a respectful distance, Schoenberg slowed down some
more and began to descend toward it. Not to the
citadel-city on its top; he was careful not to even
fly over that.

A few hundred meters below the walls of the
white city, a truncated pinnacle of rock rose out
of the woods something like a dwarfed and naked thumb on the side of the mountain's great
mitten-shape. After noticing this pinnacle,

Schoenberg approached it slowly, circled it closely, then hovered directly over it for some time, probing delicately at it with the sensing instruments in *Orion*'s hull. It was between twenty and thirty meters tall, and appeared to be just barely climbable. There was no sign that man or beast had ever taken the trouble to reach its flattened top.

De La Torre, now hanging into the stanchion behind the pilot's chair, offered: "I'd say that top is big enough to hold us, Oscar, even give us a little room to walk around outside the ship."

Schoenberg grunted. "That was my idea, to put her down there. We might have to cut a few steps or string a line to climb down. But on the other hand no one's going to come visiting unless we invite 'em."

After making a final close examination of the pinnacle's small mesa from only a few meters' distance, Schoenberg set *Orion* down on it. The landing struts groped outward, adjusted themselves to keep the ship level. There was indeed enough flat space on the rocky table to hold the ship securely, with a few square meters left over for leg-stretching. All aboard disembarked for this purpose at once. Even high up the weather at this tropical latitude was quite warm but the girls were fully clothed again, in view of their uncertainty about local morals and customs. Schoenberg had ordered all weapons left inside the ship.

Direct inspection confirmed that only one side of the mesa was conceivably climbable by human beings. Even on that side there were places where a few pitons or some cut-in steps, and perhaps a rope, would be needed to allow even agile folk to make an ascent or descent in reasonable safety.

"Where is everybody?" Celeste wondered aloud as she gazed beyond the intervening sea of treetops at the white walls of the city on the summit, slightly above their level.

De La Torre had binoculars out and was peering in another direction, downslope. "There're thirty or forty men, in some kind of a camp. Over there. I can just make out some of them from time to time, among the trees."

For a while there was no better answer to Celeste's question, no sign that *Orion*'s arrival or her sore-thumb presence above the landscape had been noticed. Of course the dense forest that covered most of the mountain might conceal a lot of movement. The trees, Suomi noted, looked like close analogues of common Earthly species. Maybe some mutated stocks had been imported by the early colonists. The trunks did seem to be proportionately thicker than those of most trees on Earth, and their branches tended to right-angle bends.

About half a standard hour had passed since their landing, and the six visitors had all armed themselves with binoculars, when the one visible gate in the city's high wall suddenly opened and a small party of white-robed men emerged, vanishing from sight again almost at once as they plunged into the woods.

Schoenberg had an infrared device with which he could have followed their progress beneath the canopy of leaves, but he didn't bother. Instead he placed his binoculars back in their case, leaned back and lit a cigar. Some minutes before Suomi had expected their reappearance so near at hand, the delegation from the city emerged from the woods again, this time into the clearing caused by rockfalls from the tower on which *Orion* rested.

Schoenberg at once threw down his cigar and moved forward to the mesa's edge and, with lifted arms, saluted the men below. Looking up, they returned the gesture with seeming casualness. There were half a dozen of them. The white robes of two or three were marked with different variations of purple trim.

The distance being too great for anything but shouted exchanges, the Hunterians came leisurely closer. The tall one in the lead reached the foot of the tower and began to climb. At first he made steady headway without much difficulty. About halfway up, however, a nearly sheer stretch brought him to a halt. He was an old man, his visitors saw now, despite the nimbleness with which he moved.

He looked up at Schoenberg, who stood openhanded some ten meters above him, and called: "Outworlders, Thorun and the other gods of Hunters' offer you greetings and grant you welcome."

Schoenberg made a slight bow. "We thank Thorun and the other illustrious gods of Hunters', wishing to put our thanks in such form as may seem to them most courteous. And we thank you too, who approach us as their spokesman."

"I am Andreas, High Priest of Thorun's king-dom in the world."

Schoenberg introduced the members of his party, Andreas those with him. After a further exchange of courtesies in which Schoenberg hinted that he would make some gift to Thorun as soon as he found out what was most suitable, he got around to the object of his visit. "As all men know, Hunters' is the planet most re-nowned in all the universe for the quality of its fighting men. We are told that the finest warriors of the planet are even now gathered here at Gods-mountain for a great Tournament."

"That is true in every word," said Andreas. His speech seemed to outworld ears much less accented than Kestand's had.

Schoenberg proceeded. "We crave the favor of Thorun in being allowed to witness this Tour-nament, at least in part."

Andreas did not look toward his companions waiting calmly below, but rather across the treetops to his city, as if to gather in some message. It was only a brief glance, before he said: "I speak for Thorun. It is his pleasure to grant you your request. The Tournament is al-ready in progress, but the most important rounds of fighting remain yet to be seen. The next is to be fought tomorrow."

Andreas talked a little longer with the out-worlders, promising that in the morning he would send a guide to conduct them to the fight-ing ring in plenty of time to see the day's events there. He promised them also that sometime during their stay they would be invited into the

city and entertained in Thorun's temple as
befitted distinguished guests. He acknowledged
Schoenberg's promise that a gift for Thorun
would be forthcoming. And then the priests and
the outworlders exchanged polite farewells.

During the short hike back to the city Andreas
was thoughtful and more than usually aloof. His
subordinates, walking with him, took careful
note of his mood and did not intrude upon him.

He was an old man by Hunterian standards,
scarred by a dozen serious wounds, the survivor
of a hundred fights. He was no longer a warrior
of great prowess, his muscles now suffering the
wastage of time and maltreatment. Nimble
climbing cost him much more effort than he allowed to show. The skull looked out from behind
his face more plainly with the passage of every
sixtieth-of-an-old-man's-life—what the outworlders would call a Standard Year.

In this progressive change of his facial appearance he found pleasure.

Though his legs were tired he maintained a
brisk pace and it was not long before he had led
his party back into the city.

There he brushed aside subordinates who
were waiting to entangle him in a hundred questions and disputes about the visitors. These men,
below the level of the Inner Circle, understood
nothing. Essentially alone, Andreas strode
quickly and still thoughtfully through the
network of bright, narrow streets. Servants,
artisans, soldiers and aristocrats alike all took
themselves out of his way. On the steps before
the tall outer doors of the Temple of Thorun a

pair of Inner Circle aristocrats in purple-spangled robes broke off their conversation to bow respectfully, a salute that Andreas acknowledged with a scarcely conscious nod. A courtesan alighting from her litter bowed more deeply. She was evidently the woman of some non-celibate priest below the Inner Circle. Andreas acknowledged her not at all.

In the Outer Temple the light was good, the sun coming in strongly through the hypaethrus in the roof; and here a low-voiced chant of war, to muffled drum, went up from acolytes who knelt before an altar piled with enemy warriors' skulls and captured weapons. An armed guard who stood before the entrance to the Inner Temple saluted Andreas and stepped aside, pulling the great door open for him. Broad stairs went down. The room to which they led was vast, built partially below the level of the sunlit streets outside.

Here in the Inner Temple the light was indirect and dim, filtered through many small portals. Andreas pushed aside hanging after hanging of chain mail with practiced hands, made his way across the enormous chamber. He passed a place where a single devout worshipper knelt, a fighting man with shield and sword in hand, a priest-general dressed all in white, praying silently before a tall stone statue. The statue, highly stylized, portrayed a man in smooth, tight-fitting outworlder's garb. He wore a round and almost featureless helm and had a grim, beardless face—Karlsen, a demigod of the distant past, a sword in his right hand, a stick-

like outworld weapon in his left. Andreas' face
was set like stone. But to have the statue removed would cause trouble. Karlsen was still a
popular figure with many of the people.

From this point on the way Andreas took was
not open, or even known, to more than a very
few. He went behind more chain mail curtains
into a corner where an inconspicuous passageway began. Again there were descending stairs,
dimmer and much narrower than before. At the
bottom a small oil lamp burned in a wall niche,
giving enough light to enable a man to walk
without groping, no more. Here were the tall
and massive doors that led to Thorun's hall.
From behind these doors at times came flaring
lights, the sound of harp and drum and horn and
booming laughter. At these times novices were
allowed to stand wide-eyed at the foot of the
stairs and briefly watch and listen, observing
from afar the evidences of gods and heroes at
feast within.

Andreas carried one of the two keys that could
open the doors of Thorun's hall. Lachaise, Chief
Artisan of the Temple and, of course, a member
of the Inner Circle, had the other. A door swung
open for Andreas now, when he turned his key in
the proper secret way, and he quickly stepped
through and pulled the door tightly shut again
behind him.

The Great Hall of Thorun, carved out of the
living rock beneath the Temple, was perhaps five
meters long, three wide, three high—certainly
modest enough in all conscience for the master of

the world. The walls, floor, and ceiling were
rough, bare stone; Thorun's hall had never been
finished. Quite likely it never would be. Work on
it had begun, he supposed, almost twenty Hunterian years ago, five times an old-man's-lifetime.
A little work had still been done in the tenure of
the previous High Priest. But since then plans
had changed. The place was big enough already
to fill its only real function; duping novices.
There was an air passage above so that bright
torches could be burned to cast their light out
under and around the doors, there were musical
instruments piled in a corner. As for the booming, godlike laughter—either Thorun or Mjollnir
could do that.

Thorun was in his hall, seated at a table that
nearly filled the inadequate room. So huge was
he that, even though seated, his eyes were on a
level with those of the tall priest standing before
him. Thorun's head of wild dark hair was bound
by a golden band, his fur cloak hung about his
mountainous shoulders. His famed sword, so
large that no man could wield it, was girdled to
his waist. His huge right hand, concealed as
always in a leather glove, rested on the table and
held a massive goblet. Seen in the dim light,
Thorun's face above his full dark beard might
have been judged human—except that it was too
immobile and too large.

Thorun did not move. Neither did the demigod Mjollnir, seated at another side of the table,
head bound in a silver band, wrapped in his dark
cloak. Of nearly equal size with the god of war
and the hunt, Mjollnir shared Thorun's foodless

and drinkless feast in gloomy comradeship.

After entering the room Andreas had waited
for a little while, standing motionless, watching
—making sure neither of them was going to be
triggered into movement by his entry. Sometimes they were. One had to be careful. Satisfied,
he walked around the high table and passed behind the chair of Thorun. There in the wall was
set a small and secret door for which no key was
necessary. Andreas opened this door by pressure
in the proper place. Behind it another narrow
stone stair wound down.

The descent was longer this time. At the bottom of the final stair Andreas turned first to his
left. After three or four strides in that direction
he emerged from a narrow tunnel to stand on the
bottom of an enormous pit dug out of the rock
beside the Temple. The excavation of this pit
had consumed in labor the lifetimes of many
slaves, having been started during the tenure of
the fifth High Priest to hold office before Andreas; so farseeing and magnificent were the
plans, now coming to fruition, of the true god!
At its top the pit was surrounded by white stone
walls and covered by a roof, so that it looked
from the outside merely like one more building
in the Temple complex, in no way remarkable
amid the maze of structures that all looked more
or less alike.

Andreas went back into the tunnel and followed it back in the direction that led right from
the foot of the stair. Before entering the doorless
chamber to which this passage brought him, he
paused and closed his eyes in reverent imitation

of Death, murmured a brief private prayer. Certainly not to Thorun. Thorun was a thing, a tool, part of a necessary deception practiced on the masses, a deception that Andreas had left behind him in the Temple. What now lay ahead was, for him, the ultimate—the only—reality.

The chamber Andreas now entered was as old as anything made by man on Hunters' planet, Dim daylight lit it now, filtering indirectly down through an overhead shaft open at some high place to the sunlight and barred by heavy grills at many places along its length. It was a little larger than Thorun's hall above. A hundred people might have squeezed themselves into this room but never had. Fewer than ten people now even knew of its existence.

Against the wall opposite the single doorway stood a low wooden table bearing a half dozen boxes of bright metal. Each box was of a different shape, and each rested in a depression or socket carved to its shape in the dark panels of the tabletop. The outer surfaces of the boxes were precisely machined and shaped, products of a finer technology than any sword-making smithy. Tubes and cables of smooth gray and black ran among the boxes in a maze of interconnections.

On second look the wooden frame supporting the boxes was not really a table, but something more like a litter or sedan chair, though not made to accommodate the human form. From opposite ends of the litter extended pairs of sturdy carrying arms with carven grips, so six or eight humans could bear the whole assembly.

The carrying handles were worn with long usage, but the litter, like the rest of the chamber,
was very clean.

The pale stone of the floor shone faintly in the
dim light. Only the low stone altar in the center
of the room was darkened by old and in-
eradicable stains, rust from the inset iron rings
to which victims' limbs were sometimes bound,
rust-colored old blood at the places over which
the victims' organs were removed. Before the litter, like fruit, the skulls of babies filled a bowl.
Offerings of flowers lay scattered in small heaps,
never in vases. Nearly all of the flowers were
dead.

After he entered the room Andreas lowered
himself to his knees, then down and fully prostrate on the floor, head and outstretched arms
pointing toward the altar and beyond it to the
litter with its metallic burden.

"Arise, Andreas," said a steady, inhuman
voice. It came from among the metal boxes,
where a small wooden frame stood on its side
holding a stretching drumskin. In the center of
the drumskin a small gleam of metal showed.
The voice produced by the drumskin was seldom
loud, though a similar device had been put inside Thorun to let him bellow and laugh. This,
the quiet voice of Death, was more like a drum-
sound than anything else Andreas had ever
heard—and yet it was not very like a drum.

Andreas arose and came around the altar, approached the litter, once more made obeisance
to the boxes on it, this time only on one knee.

"Oh, Death," he said in a soft and reverent voice, "it is truly a starship, and its pilot chose to land on the rock where you in your wisdom foresaw that such a ship might land. I am going shortly to prepare Mjollnir for his task, and to choose soldiers to go with him. I have already carried out your other orders in every particular."

The drum-voice asked: "How many outworlders came with the ship?"

"I have seen six, and there is no evidence that others are aboard. Wonderful is your wisdom, oh, Death, who could predict that such men would be lured across the sky to watch our Tournament. Wonderful and—"

"Was there any mention of the man, the badlife, named Johann Karlsen?"

"No, Death." Andreas was a little puzzled. Surely the man Karlsen must be long since dead. But the god Death was wise beyond mere human understanding; Andreas had long since been convinced of that. He waited worshipfully for another question.

After a brief silence it came. "And they are private hunters? Poachers by their own laws?"

"Yes, Lord Death, their spokesman said they had been hunting. No one in their outworld government will know that they are here."

Prompted by occasional further questions Andreas spoke on, telling in some detail all that he had so far managed to learn about the visitors and their spacecraft.

He was certain it would not be too big to fit into the pit beside the Temple.

VI

On the day after *Orion*'s landing, Leros led the sixteen Tournament contenders who were still alive up the mountain to a new and higher camp. There, when routine matters had been gotten out of the way, he read the pairings for the third round of the Tournament:

Bram the Beardless of Consiglor
Charles the Upright

Col Renba
Farley of Eikosk

Giles the Treacherous
Hal Coppersmith

Jud Isaksson
LeNos of the Highlands

Mesthles of the Windy Vale
Omir Kelsumba

Polydorus the Foul
Rahim Sosias

Rudolph Thadbury
Thomas the Grabber

Vann the Nomad
Wull Narvaez

The priest of the Inner Circle who had come
down from the city yesterday had informed
Leros and the warriors that they could expect a
group of outworlders to appear today. The
Tournament was to go on almost as usual, and
the utmost courtesy was to be shown the outworlders. If they behave strangely, ignore it.
There will probably even be women among
them; pay no attention to that, either. Leros was
also instructed to call frequent recesses in the
fighting for prayer and ceremony.

The warriors had little thought to spare for
anything that did not directly concern their own
survival in the Tournament, and the arrival of
the visitors and their guide when Leros was halfway through reading the lists caused no inter-
ruption. Four visitors came, and two of them
were women but, Leros noted with some relief,
modestly dressed. He had heard some tall tales
of outworld ways. He was not pleased to have
such onlookers—but perhaps Thorun was, for
some obscure and godly reason. In any event,
orders were orders, and Leros had endured
harder ones than this.

This day's fighting ring had been stamped out
at the head of a gentle slope in an area where the
trees were thin. From the ring the outworlders'
ship was readily visible a few hundred meters

away on its truncated pinnacle of rock. The massive ball of bright metal that carried folk out among the stars showed a single open doorway in its otherwise featureless surface. Two more outworlders were sometimes visible, tiny figures sitting or standing on the little lip of rock before the ship.

Athena, standing at ringside beside Schoenberg and waiting somewhat nervously for the action to begin, whispered to him: "Are you sure this is going to be fighting for keeps?"

"That's what our guide tells us. I expect he knows what's going on." Schoenberg was watching the preparations with keen interest, not looking at her when he answered, low-voiced.

"But if what he told us is true, each of these men has already been through two duels in this tournament. And look—there's hardly a mark on any of them."

"I can see a few bandages," Schoenberg whispered back. "But you may have a point." He considered the matter. "It could well be this: fighting from an animal's back apparently isn't done here. Therefore men have to move around strictly on their own muscle power, and can't wear a lot of heavy body armor. So a clean hit from any type of weapon is going to leave a serious wound, not just a minor gash or bruise. Most wounds are serious, and the first man to be disabled by a serious wound is almost certainly the loser. Ergo, winners don't show up for the next round with serious wounds."

They fell silent then, since Leros was looking in their direction and perhaps was ready to get

the action started. Two men with weapons ready
were facing each other from opposite sides of the
ring. De La Torre and Celeste also became utterly attentive.

Leros cleared his throat. "Bram the Beardless
—Charles the Upright."

Suomi, standing atop the mesa beside
Barbara Hurtado and looking toward the ring
from there, was too far away to hear Leros call
the names, but through his binoculars he saw
two men with raised weapons start toward each
other across the fighting ring. He put the
binoculars down then and turned away, wonder-
ing how in the universe he had managed to get
himself involved in this sickening business. For
hunting animals one could find or fabricate some
reason or excuse, but not for this—and there was
Athena, over at ringside, an avid observer.

"Someone should do an anthropological
study," she had explained to him just a little
while ago, while getting ready to leave the ship.
"If they're really fighting each other to the death
over there." Their guide-to-be, a tall, white-
robed youth, had just been explaining the Tournament to them in some detail.

"You're not an anthropologist."

"There isn't a professional one here. Still, it's
a job that should be done." She went on getting
ready, clipping a small audiovideo recorder to
her belt, next to the hologram camera.

"Is Schoenberg here to do an anthropological
study too?"

"Ask him. Carl, if you hate Oscar so much
and can't stand to look at life in the raw—why

did you come along on this trip? Why did you get me to ask Oscar to invite you?"

He drew a deep breath. "We've been through that."

"Tell me again. I would really like to know."

"All right. I came because of you. You are the most desirable woman I have ever known. I mean more than sex. Sex included, of course—but I want the part of you that Schoenberg has."

"He doesn't *have* me, as you put it. I've worked for Oscar five years now, and he has my admiration—"

"Why your admiration?"

"Because he's strong. There's a kind of strength in you too, Carl, a different kind, that I've admired also. Oscar has my admiration and often my companionship—because I enjoy his company. He and I have had sex together a few times, and that, too, has been enjoyable. But he doesn't *have* me. No one does. No one will."

"When you come of yourself as a free gift, then someone will."

"No one."

Bram and Charles were sparring cautiously in the day's first duel, neither of them having yet decided on an all-out rush. Though they were of a height Charles the Upright was much leaner, his back so straight that the reason for his name was obvious. He wore a loose jacket of fine leather and had a darkly handsome face.

Athena thought he showed incredible poise, waiting with his long, sharp-looking sword lifted in one hand, aimed at his opponent. Surely, she thought, this was not life-and-death after all. No

matter how seriously they took it, it must be
some play, some game, with a symbolic loser
stepping aside . . . and yet all the time she was
telling herself this she knew better.

"Come," Charles was murmuring, sounding
like a man urging on some animal. "Come. Now.
Now."

And beardless Bram, all youth and freakish
strength, came on, first one step, then two, then
in an awesome rush, his sword first raised then
slashing down. The sharp blades rang together,
the two men grunted. Incoherent cries of excitement went up around the watching circle.
Charles, fending off blow after blow, was giving
way now. He seemed to lose his footing momentarily in a slip, then lashed out with a coun-
terstroke that brought a hoarse noise of appreciation from the warriors who stood watching
with knowledgeable eyes. Bram avoided the
blow and was unhurt but his rushing attack had
been brought to a standstill. Athena for the first
time began to realize that fine skill must reign
here on the same throne with brutality.

Bram stood quietly for a moment, frowning as
if at the unexpected resistance of some inanimate
object. Then suddenly he charged again, more
violently if possible than before. The long swords
blurred and sang together, sprang apart, blurred
and sang again. Athena began now to see and
understand the timing and strategy of the
strokes. She was forgetting herself, her eyes and
mind opening more fully for perception. Then all
at once, somehow—for all her concentration she
had not seen how—Charles's sword was no longer in his hand. Instead it sprouted between

Bram's ribs, the hilt firmly affixed before Bram's breastbone, half a meter of blade protruding gory and grotesque from his broad back.

Bram shook his head, one, two, three times, in what seemed utter disbelief. Athena saw it all with great clarity and it all seemed very slow. Bram was still waving his own sword, but now he seemed unable to locate his newly disarmed opponent, standing in plain sight in front of him. Suddenly, awkwardly, Bram sat, dropped his weapon and raised a hand to his face, brushing at it as if struck by the thought that now his beard would never grow. The hand fell limp and Bram slumped farther, his head tilting forward on his chest. The pose looked incredibly uncomfortable, but he bore it without complaint. Only when a gray-clad slave limped forward to drag the body to one side did Athena fully understand that the man—the boy—had died before her eyes.

Charles the Upright extracted his sword with a strong pull and held it out to another slave for cleaning—while yet another spilled sand over the place where Bram had spilled his life. In the background someone was digging. The world had changed in the space of a few moments, or rather Athena had been changed. Never again would she be the same.

"Col Renba—Farley of Eikosk."

The man who started forward at the name of Col Renba was big, brown, and shaggy. He stood near the center of the arena whirling a mace, a spike-studded ball on the end of a short chain, and waited for Farley to come after him.

Oscar was saying something to her, but there

was no time to listen or think, no time for anything but watching. No time for Oscar, even.

Farley of Eikosk, fair and freckled, tall and
well made if not exactly handsome, came tread-
ing catlike in fine leather boots. His other
garments were simple, but of rich sturdy cloth.
He squinted in the sun that shone on the fine
polished steel of his sword and knife. Holding a
weapon in either hand, he feinted an advance to
within striking range of the mace, and nodded as
if with satisfaction when he saw how rapidly the
spiked weight on its taut chain arched out at him
and back again.

Now Farley began to circle, moving around
Col Renba first one way and then the other. The
mace came out after him, faster than before,
faster than had seemed possible to Athena, and
she cried out, unaware that she did so. Again she
cried out, in relief this time, when she saw that
the spikes had missed Farley's fine, fair skin.

Momentarily both men were still, and then
again there came a rapid passage of arms, too
fast for Athena to judge. She thought the flurry
was over, when suddenly the tip of one of the
mace's spikes touched Farley on the hand, and
his dagger flew lightly but awkwardly away. In
almost the same moment Farley's long sword bit
back, and now Col Renba backed away, keeping
the mace twirling with his right hand, his left
arm curled up as if trying to protect itself from
further damage while its sleeve rapidly drenched
red.

Each man's left arm was bleeding now, and
Farley's at least appeared no longer usable.
Along the back of his hand there showed the

white of splintered bone. The bright blade of his long dagger lay buried in the dust.

When the mace-spinner saw the extent of the damage he had inflicted, and found that his own left arm could at least be held up out of the way, he stopped backing off and began to advance once again. He kept the ugly weight of death moving around him in a smooth ellipse. As Col stepped closer, Farley began to retreat, but only began. As the mace sighed past him his long speed-thrust to the throat caught Col stepping in. Col Renba died, the mace flying wide from his hand in a great arc, spinning over the shouting, dodging ring of watchers.

A long moment after the other watchers' outcries had died away, Athena was still shouting. She realized this and shut up and let go of Schoenberg, whose arm and shoulder had somehow come into her spasmodic two-handed grip. Oscar was looking at her strangely, and so was De La Torre, who stood with his arm around a bored-looking Celeste a little distance off.

But Athena forgot about them. Already men were getting ready to fight again.

"Giles the Treacherous—Hal Coppersmith."
Coppersmith was the leaner of this pair, and much the taller. He was content to begin on the defensive, holding his long sword like the sensing organ of some giant insect. Giles the Treacherous had sandy hair, an air of earnest perseverance, and (like the most successful traitors, thought Athena) an open trustworthiness in his face. He was not big, and did not appear to be exceptionally strong, but still maneuvered his

own long blade with an assured economy of effort. Now it was high, now low, without Athena being aware that it had started to move. Hal Coppersmith had similar difficulties, it seemed. His elbow was gashed, and then his knee, and then the great muscle in his tattooed upper arm was cut nearly through. Then nothing remained but butchery. Giles stepped back with an expression of distaste. A slave limped forward to swing a maul and end Hal's silent, thrashing agony.

"Jud Isaksson—LeNos of the Highlands."

LeNos sprang to the attack almost before the signal had been given, his fierce scarred face thrust forward like a shield. In either hand he held a wide blade, moving and flashing like the hub-knives on a chariot. And little Isaksson, whooping as if he were overjoyed to meet a fighter so aggressive, shot forward fast enough to clash with LeNos almost in the middle of the trodden circle. The round metal shield on Jud's left arm rang like some maddened blacksmith's anvil under the barrage of his enemy's blows. LeNos seemed incapable of imagining a defensive move, let alone performing one. He only pushed his own two-handed attack so maniacally that it seemed impossible for his opponent to find a sliver of time and space in which to counterattack.

At such a pace the fight could not and did not last long. LeNos's driving sword arm was suddenly stilled, pinned in mid-air on the long, thick needle of Isaksson's sword. The highlander's dagger kept flashing on, but still Jud's bright-scarred shield took the blows. Then Jud yanked his sword free, of the ruined arm as he did, and brought it back, hacking, faster and faster, with a violence wilder if anything than his opponent's had been. LeNos was in several pieces before he died.

"What's the matter?" An insistent voice had repeated the question to her several times, Athena realized. Schoenberg was gripping her firmly by both arms, and giving her a slight shaking. He was looking closely into her face. When her eyes focused on his, the expression in his changed from concern to an odd mixture of amusement and contempt.

"Nothing's the matter. What do you mean? I'm all right." She kept looking for the next fight to start, and then realized that the priest in charge, Leros or whatever his name was, must have just ordered a recess. Slowly she realized that she had come near losing herself in the excitement of the fighting, temporarily losing control of her own behavior as if with drugs or sex. But no, it was all right. A near thing, but she still controlled herself.

Schoenberg, still looking at her with some concern, said now: "We had better give Carlos and Barbara a chance to see a thing or two."

"Him?" she laughed abruptly, contemptuously. "This isn't for him. Thank you for bringing me, Oscar."

"Nevertheless I think you've had enough."

De La Torre peered around Oscar at her. "I have, too, for the time being. Shall we walk back to the ship, Athena?"

"I'm staying."

Her tone was such that neither of the men made any further argument. Celeste meanwhile had moved next to Schoenberg; she was watching him more than what was going on in the ring. "I'm going, then," said De La Torre, and he was off.

Suomi, having handed over his sentry's rifle to De La Torre, slid and clambered down the steep slope from the mesa's top, holding on to the retractable rope that they had secured at the top to make the climb less dangerous. On this one face of the mesa the slope for the most part was not quite precipitous; there were some patches of gravelly soil and a bush or two. Already a visible path was being worn.

When he reached the level of the forest Suomi set off immediately in the direction of the tournament. Athena was there, not just for a quick look, but remaining there by choice to see it all. A purely scientific interest? Anthropology? She had never been enthusiastic on that subject before today, not around Suomi anyway. Maybe the tournament wasn't, after all, as murderous a business as he had been led to believe. Neither Suomi nor Barbara had watched. De La Torre, coming back, had said nothing about it and Suomi had not asked him. But maybe it was just as bloody as the guide had warned them, and she was still there taking it in. If she was like that, he had better know about it.

Nothing horrible was going on in the ring as he emerged from the forest and drew near. People were simply standing about, waiting, while a white-robed man went through some kind of cere-

mony before a simple altar. As Suomi came up
Schoenberg nodded a greeting to him. Athena
gave Suomi a preoccupied look. She was upset
about something, he thought, but she gave no
indication of wanting to be elsewhere. His attention was soon pulled away from her.

"Omir Kelsumba—Mesthles of the Windy
Vale."

On springy legs massive as tree trunks
Kelsumba moved forward, black skin gleaming,
axe cradled almost like an infant in his awesome
arms. Mesthles, spare and graying, thoughtful-
looking, somewhat battered by time like the ancient scythe with which he meant to fight, kept
at a respectful distance from Kelsumba for a little while, retreating with economical movements, studying the movements of his foe. Now
the axe came after him, startling Suomi with its
speed, and with such power and weight behind it
that it seemed nothing human should be able to
turn the blow aside. Mesthles made no mistakes,
had his scythe-blade in the right place to turn
the axe, but the jarring impact when the blades
met came near to knocking Mesthles down. Another axe-blow fell on the scythe, and then another. Mesthles could not get into position to
strike back. After the fourth or fifth parry, the
scythe-blade broke. A groaning murmur, like the
foretaste of blood, came up from the ring of
watchers, and Suomi heard part of it coming
from Athena. He saw the moist-lipped rapture
on her face as she watched the fight, oblivious to
him and all else.

Broken weapon still tightly in his grip, its
jagged blade still dangerous, Mesthles main-

tained his calm, and showed more agility than
his appearance suggested. For some time he
avoided being pinned against the side of the
fighting ring. Neither he nor any of the other
fighters ever seemed to consider stepping across
that simple line and outside the ring, any more
than they would consider jumping through a
wall.

The axe now came after Mesthles in what
looked like a continuous blur, seeming to pull its
giant owner after it. It struck Mesthles at last,
full in the back, as he twisted his body in trying
to dodge it yet again. His fallen body continued
jerking, twitching, moving. A slave limped forward with a maul and dealt the finishing blow.

Suomi's gut worked suddenly, labored
wretchedly, rejected in a spasm what remained
of the little he had taken for his breakfast. I
should have tranquilized myself, he thought. It
was too late now. He faced away from the ring
but could do nothing more before the vomit
came. If he was desecrating holy ground, well,
they would have to kill him for it. But when he
straightened up it seemed that no one was
paying him any attention at all. Whether it was
delicacy or lack of interest he could not tell.

"Polydorus the Foul—Rahim Sosias."

Suomi found that he could watch. Polydorus,
looking no more foul than his competitors, bran-
dished a battered sword with obvious strength
and energy. Sosias was paunchy and short, yet
he somehow managed to draw first blood with
his scimitar, making an ugly slice among
Polydorus's left shoulder. Polydorus was
galvanized rather than weakened by the injury,

and pressed an attack so hard that for a few moments it seemed he might prevail. But then he aimed a long thrust poorly, and stood looking down at his own right hand and forearm where he had just stepped on it. He grimaced and spat toward Sosias before the scimitar came back to take his life.

The white-clad priest was in the ring again, and it appeared there was going to be another recess. Not that it mattered to Suomi. He turned away, deliberately this time. He had found out that he could watch whatever further maiming might occur; but still he much preferred not to watch.

He stepped closer to Schoenberg and Athena, managed to catch the eye of the former but not the latter, and said: "I'm going back to the ship." He glanced at Celeste, but she only gave him a bored look and moved a little closer to Schoenberg.

Suomi turned away from them all and trudged back among the trees. It was good to be briefly alone again, but here in this alien forest was no place to stop and think.

When he got back to the foot of the mesa, he found that the climbing rope had been pulled up. Not in the mood to try the ascent without it, Suomi called out. A few seconds later De La Torre's head and bare shoulders appeared at the top of the slope. "What's up?" he called down.

"I've seen enough. Throw down the rope."

"All right." In a moment the rope came snaking down.

When Suomi got to the top he saw that

Barbara lay naked on a foam mattress so close to
the climbing path that De La Torre could sit on
the mattress beside her and do acceptable sentry
duty. Suomi noticed also that a pair of
binoculars had been set up on a tripod beside the
mattress in such a way that a man lying there,
perhaps with a woman beneath him, could observe uninterruptedly what was going on in the
fighting ring.

De La Torre apparently was finished for the
time being with binoculars, mattress, and girl;
he had pulled on a pair of shorts already and was
continuing to dress. His voice was mild and lazy.
"I'll turn the rifle back to you, then, Carlos, and
go down again myself."

Before Suomi had gotten the rifle's still-un-
familiar strap adjusted to fit his shoulder, De La
Torre was gone again. Suomi watched him out
of sight, then said to Barbara, who still lay
curled up tiredly on her mattress: "And how are
things with you?"

She moved a little, and said in a small voice:
"Life appears possible." Never had he seen
Barbara so obviously depressed before. He had
lain with her a couple of times on the long trip
out, and with Celeste a couple of times. Not with
Athena, though, on the trip out he could no
longer be casual with her. Now perhaps he
could.

Barbara was the only one of them who had
refused to watch the tournament at all. So of
course the sadist De La Torre had had to pick
her for his object, his receptacle ... Suomi
wanted to say something good to her but could
think of nothing. Tomorrow her nakedness

might arouse his own lust again but right now it
only made her seem defenseless and pitiable,
lying there face down. So, she had wanted to
come along on a luxurious space voyage with a
billionaire, and her wish had been granted. She
was earning her passage.

No need to walk a sentry's route around the
ship; there was only the one route by which one
could ascend. Standing at the head of the path,
looking out over the treetops without binoculars,
Suomi could see De La Torre arriving at the side
of the fighting ring. The next duel had still not
gotten underway, evidently; there were still four
men waiting to fight, if Suomi was reading the
arrangement of the distant figures correctly.
The binoculars were handy but he did not care
enough to pick them up. Perhaps he did not
want to acknowledge their present positioning
by moving them.

It promised to be a long few days ahead, until
the Tournament slaughtered itself into extinc-
tion, and then a very long trip home. But there
were compensations. It had been made clear
that whatever had seemed to be growing between him and Athena had no real existence. It
was not over—it had never been.

Barbara was sitting up and doing things with
her fingers to her hair, not yet in a mood to talk.
Suomi, turning to look to the north from this
high place, saw or thought he saw the mountainous glaciers of hunting country looming just
over the horizon there, like unsupported clouds.

What was that sound, just now? The path was
clear. Some small animal or flying creature,
then. Never mind.

Well, things were no doubt going to be social-
ly uncomfortable on the trip home, but it was
well worth it to have settled the thing between
them that might otherwise have dragged on
much longer. You had to consider this a favorable conclusion. If they had . . .

Did they have woodpeckers here? He couldn't
see the bird anywhere but still the sound came
almost continuously. Must be down under the
treetops somewhere. There was also a faint
polyphonic roar from the direction of the Tournament, what must have been a loud yell to be
audible this far away, but he did not try to see
what had happened there.

Barbara was standing up, her clothes in hand.
"I'm going in for a shower, Carlos."

"All right." He watched her walk away.
Women. Magnificent, but who could understand them?

And then, while on the subject of magnif-
icence, there had been the animal, the glacier-
beast, whose power and beauty had frozen
Suomi in awe and terror as it charged down
upon him. He now felt, surprisingly, some small
regret that he had not killed it. Better, of course,
if it had been allowed to live . . . yet, what was it
Thoreau had written? There is a time in the lives
of nations, as of individuals, when the best
hunters are the best men. Something like that.
The nation of interstellar man had presumably
long since passed that stage, of course. And so
had Carlos Suomi in his individual life. Or he
should have. Schoenberg, on the other hand,
though something more than a mere sadist—

In his mind the perception of the nagging tap-

ping sound clicked suddenly into place with a
remembered visual image, that of stone being
worked by hard metal, more precisely that of
steps being cut in the side of the mesa by
Schoenberg, hanging on the rope with moun-
taineers' implements in hand. Suomi had not
made the connection before because the sounds
he was now hearing were too rapid. No one
could wield a hammer at such a speed. And at
the same time they sounded too irregular to be
made by an automatic tool.

The climbable face of rock was still unoc-
cupied. Suomi had started around the ship to
check the other sides of the mesa when he beheld
in front of him someone, something, climbing
carefully up over the rim and into sight. A huge
head of wild, coarse, dark hair, bound by a silver
band. Beneath the head a massive wrestler's
body coming up over the edge of the cliff, clothed
in rough furs under a swirling dark cloak. On
second look the figure was so huge the mind
wanted to refuse belief.

The climber rolled the great length of his
frame out onto the horizontal surface of the mesa
and raised his gigantic head to look straight at
Suomi. The impassive face, its lower half masked
by wild dark beard and mustache, was of the
right size to fit the head, and yet it was subtly
wrong. Not that it was scarred, or intrinsically
deformed. Though it was no mask in the ordinary sense, it was yet artificial. Too skillfully
artificial, like the work of some mad artist, convinced he could fool people into thinking that
this robot, this dummy, was a man.

The figure rose gracefully to its feet and Suomi

saw something that its body had obscured. At
the very edge of the cliff a climber's piton had
been hammered into the rock. The end of a line
was knotted to an eye in the piton and the line
went tautly back out of sight over the cliff. Now
the face of a second climber, this one of normal
stature, indubitably human, rose into view.

Meanwhile the trailblazing giant had risen to
his full height. He was taller than anyone Suomi
had ever seen. As he stood up he thrust a
mountaineer's hammer into a pouch at his waist
and with the same motion of his arm unsheathed
an enormous sword.

Suomi had come to a dead stop, not paralyzed
with fear as he had been by the glacier-beast, but
simply unable to form any satisfactory explanation for what his senses were recording.

The first answer to cross his mind was that
this was all some ugly and elaborate practical
joke arranged by Schoenberg or De La Torre but
he realized even before the idea was fully formed
that they would hardly think it necessary to go to
so much trouble to scare him. And Schoenberg,
at least, would have too much sense to yell boo at
a nervous man with a loaded weapon.

The second explanation to pop into Suomi's
head was that there must be hooligans on
Hunters' planet the same as everywhere else,
and some of these had come to see what they
might steal from the outworlders' ship.

But the marauders' giant leader was not covered by either of these hypotheses. The mind
stopped and boggled at the sight, then tried to go
around it and proceed.

With some vague idea of scaring off bandits,

Suomi began to unsling the rifle from his back. As he did so the incredible giant took two steps toward him with its sword upraised, then halted as if satisfied with its position.

By this time the second climber, a Hunterian warrior, young and tough-looking, was completely up on the cliff-top and proceeding with drawn sword toward the open hatchway of the ship. The third, also of normal size, was right behind him.

"Halt," said Suomi, conscious even as he spoke of the uncertainty in his own voice. He felt foolish when no one halted even though the rifle was now in his hands.

Now there were two human invaders on top of the mesa besides the man-shaped giant, and another armed man was climbing into sight. The ship's hatch stood open and—except for Suomi—unprotected. And Barbara was in there.

He had not leveled the rifle at them yet, but now he did, and shouted "Halt!", this time with conviction. Instantly the huge figure lunged toward him, faster than any human could conceivably move. The man-slicing sword was held high, ready to strike. Suomi squeezed the trigger, realized when it failed to move that he had failed to release the safety. Instinctively he stepped back from the onrushing sword and felt his foot move into empty air. His left hand, grabbing wildly for support, caught hold of the climbing rope and saved him from a killing fall. The misstep dropped him only a short distance down from the edge of the mesa, but still his heel came down on rock with an impact that jarred his leg and spine. His arm twisted with the fall

and the rope slipped from his grip. He lost all
footing, tumbled and rolled on gravel, and
stopped when he came up with a breathtaking
slam against an outcropping of rock. Still he was
only about halfway down the path, the steepest
part of which was just below him.

With his back against the rock that had
stopped him, he half sat, half lay there, facing up
the hill. Dazedly he realized that he was not seriously injured, and that his right hand still held
the rifle. Now his finger found the small safety
lever beside the breech and turned it back.
Somehow he even remembered to set it for full
automatic fire.

The giant man-thing with its sword upraised
reared into view above. When it saw Suomi it
dropped itself onto the steep slope with the grace
of a dancer. With sword leveled at him now it
descended upon him, moving under perfect control, one long bounding stride, two . . .

The rifle stuttered in Suomi's hands. The
sword-brandishing golem's left arm erupted in a
spray of dry-looking particles and smoke as the
man-thing spun in an incredible pirouette, more
graceful by far than any wounded animal.
Knocked off balance and deflected from its
course by the shock of the rifle's force-packets,
the towering shape slid past Suomi and on down
the slope.

But it did not fall. In another moment, near
the bottom, it had regained full control and
stopped its slide. Then it turned and was calmly
climbing, like a mountain goat, at a fast run.
The sword, whirling and gleaming, came toward

him once again, the face below it a mask of insane serenity.

Suomi uttered a sobbing noise, a compound of
terror and frustration. In his hands the rifle
leaped and kicked, firing continuously while he
struggled to keep it aimed. The fur-clad
monster, face still without expression beneath
the silver headband, was stopped in its tracks.
Puffs of fur flew from it under the barrage, and
splinters and streaks of unidentifiable debris.
Then it was hurled back down the hill, still stag-
gering to keep its feet, black cloak alternately
furling and flying. Far at the bottom Suomi's
continuing mad fusillade pinned it like an insect,
leaping and convulsing wildly, against an im-
movable tree trunk.

A force-packet dissolved the silver headband
and half the monster's face in a gray bloodless
smear. The sword flew from its hand. With a
final, awkward, uphill lunge, the figure fell. It
rolled over on the ground and lay inert. At last
Suomi released the trigger.

Suddenly all was quiet. The sky, the mesa,
seemed to be whirling around Suomi's head. He
realized that he was sprawled precariously on
the steep slope, his head considerably lower than
his feet. One false move and he would go plunging down. He was breathing in little sobbing
gasps. Moving very carefully, still clutching the
precious rifle, he got his feet more or less beneath
him. Now he could feel a dozen cuts and bruises
from the fall.

He should get back up and defend the ship.
But the slope just above him was impossible.
How had he survived the tumble down? He must

be tougher than he had realized. His rolling descent had taken him away from the regular
climbing path. Couldn't get back to it here by
going sideways. He would have to go all the way
down and start up again on the proper route.

To get down he had to resling the rifle and
use both hands to grip the rock. In his present
state he took without thinking about them slides
and drops that would certainly have broken his
ankles if he had essayed them calmly.

At the bottom he kept his eyes on the figure of
his fallen enemy. He unslung the rifle once
again, but it was not needed. His rifle fire had
beaten the facing surface of the great tree trunk
into splinters, which had showered down with
leaves and twigs to make a patchy carpet on the
ground. On top of this carpet a giant doll lay
huddled where his violence had flung it.

Suomi, the killer, still unable to understand,
now unable to take his eyes away, came closer.
This time, too, as with the glacier-beast, there
was scattered fur, though this fur was a long-
dead dull brown instead of gallant orange.

He prodded with the rifle's muzzle, put out a
hand, moved the tattered cloak. What was left of
the thing's face was turned away. Beneath the
torn fur garments the bulky torso itself was torn
and shattered, pilling madness into the light of
day. No blood and bones this time, but wads of
stuff that might have filled a doll. Amid this stuff-
ing were disjointed metal rods and cams and
wheels, here and there a gleaming box or tube,
and running through all were complex networks

of metal cables and insulated wires with an irregular, handmade look about them. And this,
some power source. A hydrogen lamp? No, a nu-
clear fuel cell, not made to energize a robot, but
doubtless serving well enough.

He had killed, yet he had not. This corpse had
never lived, that much was certain. Now he
could look more coolly. He touched the side of
the cheek above the beard, and it felt like smooth
leather. The fur clothing over the torso had never
covered skin, only a carapace of hand-worked
metal armor. In its slight irregularities of shape
and thickness the armor reminded Suomi of a
warrior's shield he had just seen at the Tournament below. At close range the energy rifle
had opened this crude armor like an egg. Inside
were the structural parts, cables and rods and
such, also handworked, and mysteriously
jumbled with these were a few sealed boxes,
smooth and perfect in shape and finish, obviously of quite different origin than the rest . . .

He grasped at his belt. The communicator
was gone, and he realized with dismay that it
must have been knocked or scraped from its
holder at some point during his fall.

"Carlos!" It was Barbara's voice, shrill with
panic, coming from somewhere out of sight
above him. "Carlos, help—" It cut off abruptly
there.

Suomi ran to the foot of the climbing path and
looked up. In view at the top was the head of one
of the Hunterian men who had scaled the cliff.
Suomi took an ascending step; at once the man's
hands came into view, holding a short, thick bow

with arrow nocked and ready. Suomi began to
lift the rifle, and an arrow buzzed past his ear. It
brought a pang of authentic fright, but Suomi
did not shoot back. Dropping one man dead up
there was not going to help. Superior firepower
or not, Suomi was not going to be able to do
anything for Barbara, or regain the ship, without
help. It would be impossible to climb the path
with the rifle in his hands and once he slung his
weapon he would be at a hopeless disadvantage.

He must get help. Suomi turned and ran, ig-
noring signals of damage from his bruised and
bleeding legs and aching back. He headed for
the site of the Tournament to spread the alarm.
The rifle was not noisy and probably no one
there had heard the firing.

Before he had gotten fifty meters into the
trees, a line of uniformed men holding bows and
spears at the ready appeared before him,
deployed at right angles to his path, cutting him
off. A white-robed priest stood with them. The
uniformed soldiers of Godsmountain, and they
were not coming to help the outworlder against
bandits but were leveling their weapons in his
direction. "Try to take him alive," the priest said
clearly.

Suomi abruptly altered course once more,
running downhill for greater speed, angling
away from both soldiers and ship. Behind him
there were signal-like whistles and birdcall cries.

A single set of footsteps came pounding after
him, gaining ground. Suomi visualized another
robot monster. He stopped and turned, saw that
it was only a human soldier, but still fired with
deadly intent. He missed, blowing a notch out of

a tree limb above his pursuer's head. Whether wounded by splinters, stunned by concussion, or merely frightened, the man dove for cover and gave up the chase. Suomi fled. In the distance other men still whistled and signaled to one another, but the sounds grew fainter as he ran. When at last, utterly winded, he threw himself down in a dense tangled thicket, no sound came to him but his own laboring lungs and pounding blood.

VII

When Suomi walked away from the Tournament, Schoenberg noted that Athena was looking after him, an annoyed expression on her face. The two of them seemed to annoy each other, and that was about all. It was beginning to look as if nothing interesting was going to happen between them one way or another—which was just as well from Schoenberg's point of view because the girl was an invaluable worker and intensely loyal. Schoenberg would hate to lose her.

He wondered how she had become interested in a man like Suomi. He seemed like such a marshmallow, trailing her passively, failing at the hunt, trying to stay away from the Tournament on principle and failing that, then puking at the sight of blood when he did come. Of course such a miserable performance record might in some way prove attractive to a woman. Schoenberg had long ago given up trying to predict what women might do. That was one reason he liked having them around at all times; they were sure to generate surprises.

On his other side, Celeste moved a little closer

and brushed very lightly against his arm. That one was becoming tiresome. No more pretense of independence. Now she just couldn't bear to be separated from him, it seemed.

All at once he forgot about women. The recess was drawing to a close and the priest Leros had his list of names in hand and was about to read from it once more.

"Rudolph Thadbury—Thomas the Grabber."

Thadbury, with the air of a military leader, saluted both Leros and Thomas with his sword. Thomas gave his spear an indefinite wave that might or might not have been a response, then leveled it and moved forward. Schoenberg watched the action critically. He thought he was already beginning—only beginning, of course—to appreciate how a duel with edged and pointed weapons should be fought.

Since a sword has not a spear's range of attack Rudolph slid aside from the deep thrusts and hacked at the shaft of the spear when he could, trying to sever the spearhead and to move inside the spear's most effective range to a lesser distance, where the advantage would lie with the swordsman. All this was not very different from what Schoenberg had expected. He had read historians' theoretical treatments of personal combat, and had watched Anachronists on Earth playing with their dull weapons. He had never taken up one of their wooden swords, though; he did not care for playing much.

Thadbury had no success in hacking at the spear shaft, for it was bound with twisted strips of metal running lengthwise and the sword could not cut through. Nor did he get many chances to try; the Grabber was plainly a master of his chosen weapon. Rudolph could not move in to the range at which he wished to fight. Thomas kept his spear's long shaft flicking in and out, lightly as a serpent's tongue, and still used it handily to parry whenever it seemed the sword might reach his face or bulky torso. And then, suddenly, incredibly, Thomas was no longer staying back to get the maximum advantage from his weapon's greater range. Instead he brushed the sword out of the way with the spear shaft and leaped in to close with his opponent in a wrestler's grip.

A cry of surprise went up around the ring, and Thadbury too was taken off guard. Sword and spear fell to the trodden earth together and the two men stamped and whirled in a grotesque dance, each trying to trip and throw the other. But Thomas had the advantage of strength and skill as well. When they fell he was on top, Rudolph prone beneath him. Thomas's massive right forearm became a lever to crush Rudolph's wiry neck. Rudolph, belly down on the ground beneath his foe, kicked, wretched, and twisted with desperate strength. His struggles seemed useless. His face went red, then purple.

Schoenberg thought that what was left of the oxygen in his bloodstream and lungs must be going fast. He hoped the man would be speedily out of his pain, even as he pushed Celeste back a little and stepped slightly to one side to get a better look at the coming of death. He knew that a lot of people on Earth, seeing him standing here and watching so intently, would think he was a sadist. In fact, he wished no living creature suffering.

Schoenberg wished that he could enter the Tournament himself. Of course he knew full well that he was no more qualified to face such men as these with edged weapons, than they were to meet him with energy rifles. The season before, when he had been hunting with Mikenas, Mikenas had shown him how to use a hunting spear and Schoenberg had successfully impaled some dangerous game on his borrowed weapon. That had been one of the most memorable experiences of his life, and he had never mentioned it to anyone.

Of course competing in a Tournament like this was a far different matter. Not that he could reasonably expect to be allowed to enter anyway. Maybe he could find out just how one qualified in the preliminaries, and when the next planet-wide Tournament was going to be held. He assumed there would be another one, probably next hunting season. Then if he found some way to practice on Earth, and came back in fifteen years . . . maybe one of these men's sons would kill him then.

It was unlikely, to put it mildly, that he would ever be able to win a major Tournament on Hunters' planet, no matter how much practice and fair preparation he got in. He was not anxious to die, and when he saw violent death approaching he knew that, as in the past, he would be afraid. But it would be worth it, worth it, worth it. For the timeless share of intense life to be experienced before the end. For the moments of full perfect being when the coin marked Life

and Death spun before the altar of the god of
chance, moments more valuable than so many
years of the dreariness that made up most of
what men called civilization.

Now Rudolph could no longer strain to throw
his killer off, could no longer even grate out
noises from his mouth and throat. His face was
hideous and inhuman. There was no sound now
but Thomas the Grabber's honest panting. That
quieted shortly as Thomas sensed the life below
him fled. He led Rudolph's head fall, got to his
feet, very easy and limber in his movements for
such a bulky man.

Schoenberg glanced at Celeste, who was looking at her fingernails. Not horrified by what was
going on, only mildly disgusted. When he looked
at her she gave him a quick questioning smile.
He turned to Athena. She was watching the men
arm themselves for the next fight, was deep in
her own thoughts. Schoenberg and the rest of the
outside world had been forgotten.

De La Torre came ambling up, from the direction of the ship, to stand beside them. "How'd
the last one go?" he asked Schoenberg, craning
his neck a little to view the bodies where they
had been dragged.

"It went all right. They both fought well."

"Vann the Nomad—Wull Narvaez."
This should be the last fight of the day.

Athena turned her head but not her eyes to
Schoenberg and whispered: "What are those
things on his belt?"

There were two or three pairs of them, strung
on a cord. "They appear to be human ears."

De La Torre emitted a high-pitched snicker that made Schoenberg glance over at him for a moment, frowning in surprise.

Vann the Nomad was waving his long sword with what seemed to be the clumsy movements of an amateur, but nobody now watching him could be taken in by that deception for a moment. The show now became almost comical, for Narvaez, too, affected an innocent appearance. He looked so like a harmless peasant that the look must have been carefully cultivated. Wull carried a pitchfork, and made tentative jabbing motions with it toward his foe. Wull's dress was crude, and his mouth pursed grotesquely, so that he looked for all the world like some angry, mud-footed farmer nerving himself to unfamiliar violence.

The six warriors who had already survived the day's dangers were relaxed now and in a mood for humor, enjoying the charade. They hooted and whistled at clumsy-looking feints, and called out rough advice. Leros glanced around at them in irritation once, but then to Schoenberg's surprise said nothing.

With a flash of insight Schoenberg realized that the contestants in a Tournament like this one must stand closer to the gods than even a priest of Leros's rank.

Vann tried several times to cut the pitchfork's shaft, which was not armored with metal, but Narvaez had a way of turning the fork that minimized the swordblade's impact, and the wooden shaft seemed very springy and tough. When Vann's tactics had failed him several times he tried something new; grabbing at the fork with his free hand. He was so fast that on his first attempt he managed to seize the weapon, getting a good grip on it just where the tines branched out. With this grip he pulled the surprised Wul Narvaez off balance while his sword thrust low and hard.

He took the ears of Narvaez before the man was dead, warning the maul-slave off with a snarl, until he had made sure of undamaged trophies.

Athena, blinking, came back to full awareness of her surroundings once again. She looked for Schoenberg, and saw that he had turned away and was waiting to talk to the High Priest Andreas, who had just come in sight on the road that descended from the mountaintop, walking with a small escort of soldiers.

De La Torre, moving closer to Athena, asked her in a low voice: "Did you get that last little bit?"

"What?" Not having understood, she turned to him with a look of expectancy.

"I was talking about the ear-cutting, whether you got that part down on crystal. I've been making a few recordings too."

The expectancy in her face dimmed, then vanished abruptly as realization came. The crystal on which her day's anthropological records were to have been made still hung unused at her belt.

Andreas, after having made a short congratulatory speech to the surviving warriors, turned quickly to Schoenberg and inquired: "Have you enjoyed the day's competition?"

"We who are here have enjoyed it very much. I must apologize for Suomi, the one who became ill, as you may have heard. I do not think he will come to watch again."

Andreas's lip curled slightly but he made no further comment. None was needed. Such a man was beneath contempt and unworthy of discussion. He asked: "Will all of you join me at a feast in the Temple of Thorun tonight? All of you, that is, who are now here. We can ascend at once to the city if that is convenient."

Schoenberg hesitated only marginally. "I did not think to bring a gift for Thorun with me from the ship."

Andreas smiled. What was the naive old saying? If a smile disfigures a man's face, then that man is bad. The High Priest said: "I am sure you will provide a suitable gift. There is no hurry about it, not now."

"Very well." Schoenberg glanced at those of his shipmates present. All watched him expectantly and appeared perfectly ready to be Thorun's guests. "Just let me say a word to the people waiting at the ship. Only take a minute."

"Of course." Andreas, noble savage, turned politely away.

Schoenberg took his communicator from his belt and spoke into it. Looking toward the ship he thought he could just see the head of Suomi, who must be sitting down in his sentry's poistion at the top of the climbing path.

It was Barbara who answered. "Hello?" Her voice was uncertain.

"Look, Barb, those of us down here now have been invited up to visit the Temple. A feast is scheduled. I'm not sure when we'll get back to the ship. Tell Suomi to be sure to get inside before dark and button the thing up. One of you call me if any problems should arise; I'll call you again when we're ready to start back. Okay?"

There was a little pause, and then she only said, "Okay."

"Everything all right?"

"Yes. Okay, Oscar."

Just hearing about the Tournament and thinking about it must have upset her, he supposed. Probably she had been holding Suomi's hand while he recounted bestial horrors. Well, next trip he would choose his traveling companions more carefully. None of this bunch were exactly what he had hoped for.

Except next time he might be coming here alone, not expecting to return to Earth. He wondered if he could really teach himself, on Earth, to use edged weapons with real skill. He wondered if he would do better with sword or axe or spear. Tonight, if everything went well, he would have a chance to mention his plan to Andreas.

The little party of outworlders and their casual escort of a few soldiers began to climb the smooth-paved mountain road, Andreas and Schoenberg walking together in the lead. "It is only a few kilometers to the top," Andreas informed them. "Perhaps an hour's walk if we take our time. Your hours on Earth are about the same length as ours, not so?"

When they had walked only about half a kilometer along the zig-zag, climbing road they came to the place where, as Andreas pointed

out, the ring was being prepared for the next
day's fighting. Here the mountain was steeper,
less level space was available, and one side of the
ring overlooked a bank that was almost a preci-
pice. After another kilometer the switchback
road passed between twin stone watchtowers
from which sentinels saluted the party crisply
with their spears. Andreas returned the salutes.

They must be nearing the summit now. The
slope of the mountain moderated again and the
road wound through a park-like wood. Many of
the trees bore fruit. The earth below them was
hidden under a vine-like groundcover plant that
put up leaves like blades of grass.

Presently the trees thinned out, the ground
leveled and they came in sight of the citadel-city
on the mountain's crown. As the road brought
them near the city's bone-white walls, straight
toward a yawning gate, Schoenberg glanced
back once in the direction of the ship. He was
developing a faint uneasiness that he found hard
to shake. He could see only the top of the metal
sphere above the trees before he passed into the
city.

Inside, there was at first little to be seen, except more walls of bright white stone. As they
made their way in through the streets, Schoenberg found them narrow and busy. Gray-clad
slaves, and carts pulled by multihorned draft
animals, made way for white-robed aristocrats.
Here and there an elegant woman eyed the visitors from a sedan chair or a grilled window.
Windows were usually small, doors usually kept
closed, walls invariably white. There was a deadly sameness to the architecture of the city.

Catching Andreas's eye, Schoenberg asked: "May we take pictures here?"

"Of course. You must take one of me, later. I shall treasure it."

The white-garbed lords of the planet were lining the visitors' path now in considerable numbers, bowing lightly and courteously, showing somewhat more curiosity than Schoenberg had ever before seen displayed by Hunterians. Athena was smiling and waving to the women and children in white who were visible peering from windows or around corners. Those in gray, male and female, generally seemed too hurried to look up. It occurred to Schoenberg that there were no gray-clad children visible.

"The Temple of Thorun." Andreas had stopped and was pointing to a pair of high gates of heavy metal grillwork that guarded the entrance to a courtyard lined on three sides by buildings of the ubiquitous white. These were somewhat taller than any the visitors had passed on their way through the city.

"There we will feast tonight."

Once the party had passed through the gates, Andreas bade the visitors a temporary goodbye, and himself went on toward the building that Schoenberg took to be the Temple proper, the tallest structure, some twelve or fifteen meters high, with broad white steps and forbidding doors.

The outworlders were guided by bowing young priests into another nearby building and there shown to individual rooms, all of which were out of sight of the street, opening onto a kind of formal garden in an enclosed court.

Led into his room by the obsequious manservant assigned to him, Schoenberg found it a
small but pleasant place. The small window was
protected by an ornamental grill, soft rugs covered the floor, and there was a comfortable-look-
ing bed. An invitation to stay overnight seemed
to be in the cards. His manservant was laying
out white garments produced from somewhere,
and through the open door other servants were
visible, carrying in haste what appeared to be a
bathtub.

A little later, getting his back scrubbed—
hardly necessary, but let them do things their
way—he found that the unexpected degree of
hospitality had to some extent allayed the un-
ease that had begun to nag him. Now, though,
he suspected that Andreas was going to ask him
some rather large favor before they parted. What
could it be? Probably to smuggle in some outworld weapons, something needed to reduce
some particularly troublesome adversary.

The swift tropical Hunterian night had come
on by the time he had finished bathing and
dressing. A young priest was promptly at hand
to conduct him to the feast; it seemed that everything was running on a smooth schedule.

With a word to his guide he stopped at
Athena's room, next to his, and found her ready
to join him, as prompt as when they went off on
a business trip. Her guide had told her that De
La Torre and Celeste, whose rooms were next
along a covered walk, had already gone on
ahead.

Joking a little about what sort of merchandise
they might hope to sell to their new client An-

dreas, Schoenberg and Athena followed their guides from one courtyard and cloister to another without being brought again in sight of the city's streets. Evidently the Temple complex was extensive.

At last they entered a small door in the flank of the tall building Schoenberg recognized as the Temple itself and were led down to a large room a short distance below ground level. It was refreshingly cool after the day's sunlit warmth.

Already at table were De La Torre and Celeste, also garbed in white, De La Torre with a leafy garland on his head like some ancient Roman. With them sat the High Priest, and half a dozen other men all of the highest rank. Some of these had accompanied Andreas on his first welcoming visit to the outworlders' ship.

Servants moved quietly and efficiently about. The banquet room was large, pleasingly decorated with fine hangings, softly lit with well-placed candles. All was as it should be.

"Our host has been telling me about Thorun's great hall," said De La Torre, after greetings had been exchanged.

"So?" Schoenberg moved a hand around in an inclusive gesture. "Is this the place?"

One of the Inner Circle priests grinned, broadly and cynically. "No, Thorun's is really quite a different world from ours. Or yours."

As at the Tournament, Schoenberg, when seated, found himself between Athena and Celeste. Here, despite the outwardly pleasant surroundings, not only Celeste but Athena kept drawing close to him, as if unconsciously. Not

only were there no other women guests this evening, but Schoenberg had the feeling that there
might never have been any in the history of the
Temple. Andreas and the other Hunterian leaders never spoke to Athena unless she asked them
a direct question, which she did of course from
time to time to show her nerve. Celeste, being a
good playgirl, knew when she was expected to
keep quiet. If the Hunterians knew her real status, Schoenberg supposed, they would be out-
raged.

No doubt about it, his party was being ac-
corded extraordinary treatment. He would have
to at least appear to agree to their requests when
it came, whatever it might be.

The feast was elaborate and very good, though
Schoenberg with an apologetic explanation to
Andreas advised the other outworlders not to
partake of certain dishes, nor of the fermented
milk that was brought before them in great
bowls. "It will be better for our Earthly stom-
achs if we drink clear water here, if Thorun does
not object."

Andreas waved a negligent hand. "Thorun is
largely indifferent to such matters. Clear water is
always a good warriors' drink."

Schoenberg sipped his water, from a golden
cup. "I look forward to seeing the next round of
the Tournament."

"I, too. I am delighted that our interests coin-
cide. Unfortunately business has prevented me
from seeing any of the earlier rounds."

"I know what the press of business can be
like."

Celeste's foot was tapping under the table.

Dancers had come on the scene and she was watching them with professional interest. They were good, girls and youths dancing together, the show very crude by Earth standards of course, and too bluntly erotic in places, but well practiced and full of energy. The Hunterian men at table watched the show with somewhat grim expressions, or did not watch it at all. Schoenberg wondered if priests here were supposed to be celibate. He would get around to asking that later, if at all. Sex on any planet was likely to be an even more sensitive subject than religion, which these religious leaders did not appear to take too seriously.

All was new and interesting to the outworlders and the evening passed quickly for them. The night was well advanced, the candles burning low, and the dancers literally collapsed from exhaustion, when Schoenberg suggested that the time had come for him and his party to return to their ship.

Andreas made a gesture of polite disapproval. "Your beds here have been prepared. One of the dancing girls yonder will share yours with you if you like."

"The offer is most pleasing. But I am concerned about my ship."

"Stay here. Spend the night under Thorun's roof. You and I have much more to talk about. And it would be unpleasant, trying to climb the tall rock at night to reach your ship."

Schoenberg did not take long to make up his mind. "We accept your invitation gladly. If you will excuse me, though, I must talk briefly to the people on the ship." He took the communicator from his belt, activated it, waited for an answer. None was immediately forthcoming. He raised the device to his mouth and spoke. "Suomi?"

"Stay here," said Andreas, making his face hideous with his smile. "In the morning I will try to facilitate your meeting with him."

"You will try . . . I do not understand."

"You see, the man you left to guard your ship is there no longer. It is shameful but necessary to explain that while the last round of the Tournament was in progress he took fright and fled from that place. I did not wish to worry you unnecessarily, but we have not yet managed to locate him."

Schoenberg sat up straight, giving Andreas his best tycoon's look. "And what about my ship?"

"We are guarding it for you. Nothing in it will be damaged. No one can reach it, except by my authority. Come, I must insist you stay the night."

VIII

Shortly after the next morning's dawn a slave came around to waken the eight survivors of the Tournament.

Giles the Treacherous, roused instantly by the light tug on his sleeping robe, rolled over, remembered fully where he was, and came awake with something of a start. Sitting up, he rubbed sleep from his eyes and looked about him, then observed to anyone who cared to listen: "Our camp is growing somewhat smaller day by day."

Though most of the seven others were awake, none of them chose to respond immediately. Like Giles, they had simply wrapped themselves in robes or blankets for sleep, and now there was a general slow emergence, as of a gathering of insects from cocoons.

It had rained a little during the night. The morning was gray and cheerless. On the previous evening the eight warriors had bedded down quite close together, as if by common consent against some external danger. The space they now occupied was tiny indeed compared with that of the first fine encampment beside the river far below.

When Giles stood up the river was visible to

him down there, bend after bend of it snaking
across the flat country until it lost itself at last in
fields of morning mist. Down there croplands
made ragged rectangles. For a moment—a moment only—Giles wished with the intensity of
physical pain that he was somewhere in his own
remote province, striding stupidly behind a
plow, as once he had done, long ago.

Long ago.

Omir Kelsumba, giant and black, was standing a few paces away and preparing to empty his
bladder down the hill. The slaves had not gotten
around to digging a latrine for this campsite
before most of them were for some reason called
away to other duties, yesterday afternoon. Omir
spoke over his shoulder to answer Giles at last:
"Tonight we will need less space still, but what
of that? Soon all of us will be dwelling in
Thorun's hall, where there must be room
enough for any man."

"Well spoken," commended Farley of Eikosk,
standing tall to stretch, then bending and with
deft movements of his freckled arms starting to
roll up his sleeping robe. Like his weapons, it
looked costly.

By now all of the warriors were up, busy
scratching, stretching, spitting, rolling their
sleeping robes in preparation for moving camp.
Farley of Eikosk went to offer a prolonged
obeisance before the altar of Thorun, kneeling
and murmuring prayers, bending his forehead to
the ground. Soon Kelsumba joined him, and
then Charles the Upright, and then one by one
the others, until all had offered at least per-

functory worship. The enigmatic face of the little
image of Thorun showed no sign of favoring any.

Vann the Nomad was hungriest this morning,
it seemed, being first to leave the shrine and
move toward the cooking fire where a single
gray-clad slave was preparing what looked like a
very simple morning meal.

As Vann moved away, Giles said in a low
voice to Kelsumba: "What do you think of that
one, cutting ears for trophies?" Kelsumba only
grunted in reply. He had begun to inspect his
axe, checking to see if the night's rain had gotten
through its carefully wound and oiled wrappings
to rust the steel. Except for the axe, everything
Kelsumba owned was shabby and worn.

While crouching over his axe and looking at it
closely, he said to Giles: "You are perhaps a
wise man. Maybe you can give me an opinion on
this. Suppose I do not win the Tournament.
Even so, having come this far, I will be seated
high up at Thorun's table. Will he listen to me,
do you suppose? If I die today or tomorrow will
he intercede with the goddess of healing to grant
a favor for me?"

Giles gave a little private sigh. "Such a question is beyond me," he answered. "But it is generally believed that all wounds, old or new, are
healed when one enters Thorun's hall, whatever
one's rank inside."

"Oh, it is not my own wounds that have
brought me here." The big man looked up and
turned vacant eyes into the distance. "I have a
wife and two little ones, far away. The babies are
both sick, they waste and do not grow. The vil-

lage doctors can do nothing. I pleaded with the gods, offered sacrifice, but the children did not get better." His eyes swung around to Giles, and his fingers moved upon the handle of his axe. "So I will become a god myself. Then I will be able to make my children well, even if I cannot live with them any longer." His voice was rising and his look had become the stare of a fanatic. "I will kill six men, or sixty if need be! I will kill you, and Thorun himself will not be able to stop me!"

Giles nodded gravely, signifying agreement, keeping his face immobile. Then he turned carefully away. When he glanced back a moment later, Kelsumba was sitting there quietly again, honing his axe.

Thomas the Grabber, who had been standing only a little distance off when Giles made his remark about Vann's ear-cutting propensities, had probably heard the comment. It was Thomas who should be due to oppose the ear-cutter in this day's round of fighting, but Thomas, looking sleepy this morning, seemed not at all disturbed. Now he was yawning, with a kind of cavernous bellow. It was hard to say whether Kelsumba or the Grabber was the biggest of the surviving men. Jud Isaksson was certainly the smallest, with Giles not much larger. The latter sighed once more to himself as he made this assessment.

Breakfast consisted of thick tasteless fried cakes and water. For the first time there was no meat. When the men growled at the slave who served them, he indicated by a few grunts and helpless gestures—someone had once cut out his tongue—that nothing better had been provided and he was having to do more work than usual because most of his fellows had been called away.

Leros confirmed this, scowling as he munched his own share of the fried cakes. "Two priests who are my friends came down to rouse me early this morning, to sympathize with me that most of our retinue has been taken away. There is no excuse for giving us such meager service. True, our numbers are reduced, but the glory of you who survive has grown the greater. I have sent up a protest to the High Priest. I trust we will be better fed, and attended, by midday."

Breakfast, such as it was, having been disposed of, Leros gave the order to march and the party began once more to ascend. Far ahead of them a train of freight wagons loaded with provender for the city went groaning slowly up the road. Another, of empty, rattling carts, came clattering more quickly down. Charles the Upright, who happened to be walking in the van, had to reach for his sword before the surly driver of the first descending cart would lead the train of vehicles fairly off the road to let the climbing heroes pass.

Leros's irritation was increased by the incident, but he said little and the party hiked on. Certainly it was true that they no longer made an impressive sight. The men were all bedraggled after days spent in the field and they were practically unattended. He had felt like stopping to flog that insolent varlet of a driver, but such a job would only demean the whole proceeding further.

The city of Thorun was not yet visible, though

the summit of Godsmountain could hardly be more than a kilometer above them now. Once Giles caught a glimpse of the huge outworld ship, gleaming wetly on its distant pedestal of rock, but then rain and fog blew in between, and trees closed in again around the road on which they climbed.

Two priests of intermediate rank came down to meet Leros and talk with him. The three of them, conferring privately, walked on ahead of the eight warriors. The eight continued to climb calmly and steadily, sometimes two or three walking together long enough to exchange a few words, sometimes all of them strung out, each in his solitary introspective silence. A ragged pair of slaves, all that remained of their once princely retinue, bore burdens in the rear. One slave was dumb and the other limped on a crippled leg. The image of Thorun, for which a field shrine had been built at every camp thus far, had now been left behind. Temporarily, Leros said, until they should have servants again to build a decent shrine.

Shortly after the near-incident of the carts, Giles the Treacherous sought out Jud Isaksson who had been trudging alone and walked companionably beside the man who in a few hours would be trying to kill him. Jud acknowledged his presence with a glance and then went back to his own thoughts.

Casting a glance back at their beggarly force of servants, Giles remarked: "So, no meat. And it also seems there will be no musicians today, to waft our souls upward to Thorun's hall."

Jud shrugged uneasily. Perhaps it was only the wet wind blowing rain against his neck that made him do so.

Giles measured out half a dozen strides of road beneath his boots, and then added: "I know only this. Sixty-four brave fighting men, all full of life and blood and valiant deeds, met on the plain below. And now there are just eight of us with breath still in us. *Then,* when we still might have turned around and gone home, we were greeted and praised as heroes. Now? No one beholds our deeds, or will ever sing of them. And are the dead fifty-six in truth now at their feasting up above?" He looked toward the mountaintop concealed amid its groves. "I hear no sounds of laughter down the wind."

Jud's mustache moved, but he only spat.

Giles was determined not to let things drag on; time was growing short. He said, trying almost at random now to provoke a reaction: "You and I have seen those fifty-six good men go up in smoke. No, not even that. They have not all been burnt, as heroes should be, but buried for the most part like dead animals. In shallow graves."

"Man." Jud found his voice at last. "Man, I know not why you rehearse these things to me. Tell me—I know nothing of you but your name —is it for no reason at all that you are called Giles the Treacherous?"

"That is a long story, and not too easy of belief. I will begin it if you like."

"No, I care not. A true scoundrel would probably call himself Giles the Honest. All right!" Jud came visibly to a decision. "All right! If you

want plain speaking. A child should know there
are no gods on top of this mountain, or anywhere
else. That being so, who really does rule the
Temple, Godsmountain, the world? The simple
answer is, that they are ruled by men."

He nodded, smiling with satisfaction at his
own logic, and then plunged on. "Very well.
Since we're not going to be welcomed into some
imaginary hall, the question arises, why are we
here? There must be a real reason. T'would be
senseless to have us kill one another off to the last
man for the amusement of a few outworlders
who happened by. No. Mark my words. Before
this day's duelling starts—or at worst before it's
over—the six or eight of us who're left will be let
in on the secret, and the Tournament will be secretly stopped."

"You really think that."

"Man, what else? We're going into some elite,
secret force. They've already stopped sending
down supplies for us right? The Tournament
will be halted, and some story put out telling
who the final winner was and how he's happily
guzzling and wenching with the gods."

"The good Leros must be an excellent ac-
tor."

"Maybe he hasn't been told. A good man and
all that, but not the brightest. It's plain enough
if you only look at it, consider all the facts. We're
going into some kind of palace guard, for the
High Priest and whoever else is really running
things atop this mountain."

When Jud fell silent, Giles also had no more to
say for a little while, though he was thinking
rapidly. At last he replied: "You may be right. I

only know that I would give much to be able to turn my own steps quietly downhill at this moment and retrace them to my home."

"You speak madness, Giles. Once you have come this far they would never let you go. Where is your home?"

"Endross Swamp." It was a remote province, far to the south. "The writ of Godsmountain does not run there with much effect."

"So I have heard. In fact I would have thought that place was full of Thorun's enemies." Jud was staring at him. "Why are you here?"

"I am no enemy of Thorun," Giles said at once, and firmly. "It may be that some of his priests are not as worthy and honest as they should be. As to why I am here, well, I am now asking that question of myself."

Up ahead the priests had stopped, still deep in their discussion. Leros was gesturing angrily, while the other two appeared unhappy but resigned. They had reached the next ring prepared for fighting. Giles saw that it had been made with a portion of its rim overlooking an almost precipitous slope. As he stared, he felt a chill sensation near his heart. In the south they thought that meant a man had laid eyes on the place where he would die.

"What did I tell you?" Jud was murmuring, nudging Giles with an elbow. Leros had turned around as they came up, and was about to speak to the warriors. But something in Leros's attitude had changed and they all recognized at once that he was not simply going to announce another round of fighting. Something else impended.

* * *

Leros was angry, but not at the warriors, not
at the gloomy priests who stood beside him.
When he spoke his voice was tense. "First I am
instructed to ask whether, when the outworlders
were with us yesterday, any of them mentioned
the name of the demigod Karlsen."

The warriors all exchanged mildly puzzled
looks. Most of them could not remember anything the outworlders had said: they all had
more important things to think about. This was
hardly the announcement Jud had expected, and
he was frowning.

All were silent until Giles put up a hand and
asked: "Good Leros, are these outworlders then
accused of some blasphemy?"

"That is being decided up above," said one of
the other priests, gesturing toward the summit.

"Tell Andreas to decide it up there, then,"
said Leros tartly. "And let me get on with more
important business here."

"Lord Leros, your pardon. I repeat again, I
and many others are sympathetic to your views.
I am only relaying orders—"

"Yes." Again Leros addressed the waiting
warriors. "Those above see fit to bother us with
a second triviality. One of the outworlders, the
one who behaved like a frightened woman when
he saw blood, has wandered off. It is thought he
must still be on the mountain, for soldiers patrol-
ling in the flatlands have not found him. I must
ask whether any of you have caught sight of such
a person either last night or today."

Giles signed that he had not. The other seven,

by now almost totally uninterested, also gave mutely negative responses.

Leros turned back to the other priests. "Do not these outworlders carry devices for talking one to the other, even when they are kilometers apart? How can one be lost if he can tell the others where he is?"

One of the other priests said: "Such a device was found near their ship. The coward must have dropped it. Anyway, in my opinion he does not want to be found. Other even stranger things were found there also, and there is more going on than we have been told." The priest's voice dropped almost to a whisper. Giles feigned a boredom as great as that of the other fighting men around him, and he kept his eyes on a little flying creature in a tree, but meanwhile his ears grasped for every word.

The priest continued his private—he thought —conversation with Leros: "The other outworlders are said to be guests in the Temple precincts but no one believes they remain there by choice. Very few people have seen them since they entered. One of their women seems to be confined aboard their ship. More, and stranger —one that I shall not name has told me of a most surprising rumor; the demigod Mjollnir went forth to challenge the outworlders, and one of them slew him."

Leros made a disgusted sound and turned his back. "And I had been on the verge of giving credence to these stories you bring."

"Oh, I do not credit that about Mjollnir myself. Certainly not! Blasphemous. But something strange is going on, something to do with the outworlders, and we have not been told the truth about it."

"That may well be. But it has nothing to do with me or with this Tournament." Leros squinted up the road. "When may we expect better food and drink, and some new servants?"

The third priest looked unhappier than before. "Lord Leros, again I must give you an answer that you will not like."

Leros swung around. "What now?" His tone was ominous.

"It is as if the Inner Circle has suddenly forgotten about the Tournament. Not simply that they are busy with other things, but that they no longer care about it. I could get no promise that the rations sent down would be improved. Andreas I saw only briefly, and he was preoccupied with other matters, I know not what. He said to me: 'Bid Leros get on with his show, and finish up.' How can I question the High Priest?"

Leros's hand went unthinkingly to his side, where a warrior's belted sword would hang, found only the smooth white priestly robe. "My show? Were those his words?"

"On my honor, they were."

"Well, *I* can question what Andreas orders." Leros spoke in cold rage, his words quiet and calculated. "High Priest or not. What else will he take from us? Why not all our slaves and food, why not our clothes and weapons as well?" The other priests looked as if they were trying not to hear. Giles was holding his breath in concentration.

Leros went on: "Is this or is it not supposed to

be a Tournament pleasing to Thorun and worthy of him, intended to select a man who is worthy of apotheosis? Are not these eight remaining champions, each and every one, the finest . . ." Words failed Leros for the moment. Indeed he seemed near strangulation. At last he managed to draw a deep breath and resume. "Very well. I must go up and question him myself on these matters. One of you two must stay here for a while, that these men be not left unattended by any of high rank."

Turning then to the eight waiting warriors, Leros lost his scowl and faced them with a sad and loving smile. "Good lords—good men. I must leave you for a while. Do you wish to go on with this round of fighting or wait for my return? I am going up the hill to argue for better treatment. There is no telling when I will get back." The men looked at one another uncertainly. Giles almost spoke, and then bit back the words. His mind was racing, trying to balance probabilities. He wanted a delay, but not too much of one.

Leros, seeing their uncertainty, glanced at the high bronze shield that was Hunters' sun trying to burn its way through layers of mist. "Wait until the hour of noon," he told them. "If I am not back by then, with better honors and provisions for you—or have not sent word—then fight on as best you can." Handing over his list of names to the priest who had been chosen to stay with the men, and beckoning the others to come along, he started at a brisk pace up the hill.

The long morning dragged slowly by. Until

the middle of the day the warriors stood or lounged around, gloomily silent or conversing two or three together in low voices. At last, when it was plain that noon had come and gone and there had been no word from Leros and no sign of his return, the substitute priest cleared his throat and called the eight together. In a somewhat awkward little speech he introduced himself as Yelgir, and announced that he was ready to call the roll if they were prepared to fight.

"Let us get on with it," said Vann the Nomad. Others nodded their readiness. Waiting and uncertainty were harder to bear than blows. They took their places around the ring.

Yelgir took out the roll of names and cleared his throat once more. "Charles the Upright—Farley of Eikosk."

From their opposite sides of the ring Charles and Farley advanced in almost leisurely fashion. In the center they touched weapons carefully, each man showing respect for the other's abilities, and began a cautious sparring. Farley's wounded left hand, that Leros himself had neatly splinted and bandaged, did not appear to be causing him any trouble except that he opened the fight with sword alone, leaving his dagger in his belt.

Gradually the fighters added speed and strength to their movements until the long swords rang musically. The contest seemed quite even between them. Then Farley's jewel-bright steel dipped in a flashy feint he had not used in any earlier round of fighting. Charles tried to parry the stroke that did not come, and missed the deadly one that did; he fell to earth with one bright shriek of pain.

"Giles the Treacherous—Jud Isaksson."

Jud, as before, charged out quickly. Giles did not seem nearly so eager, but still this fight began at a faster tempo than had the previous one. Both men were active, but neither would commit himself utterly to an attack. Now Giles became the more aggressive; his long sword lanced above and below the smaller man's round shield, but did not manage to get around it. And now Isaksson's blows fell thick and fast and Giles was forced to spend his energy in parrying, and then to give ground before the onslaught.

The end came suddenly when Giles was backed against the rim of the fighting circle that overhung the downhill slope. Jud's blade flashed, a mere glint of light, and Giles clutched at his chest, gave a choked cry, fell. On the steep turfy incline his body slid and tumbled a score of meters before a bush caught and held it momentarily. Then it pulled loose and slid on again. The priest beckoned. The limping slave with the maul began the long climb down.

"Omir Kelsumba—Rahim Sosias."

The black giant seemed to grow even larger upon entering the ring. Again he carried his great axe cradled in his two arms almost tenderly. Against him, fat Sosias with his curved sword looked terribly overmatched. But the scimitar drew first blood. It was a light wound, a mere touch with the point along the outside of Kelsumba's thigh. Sosias's timing had been perfect; the riposte with the axe only tore the edge of his loose outer garment.

The wound galvanized the black man, and

now Sosias had to go jumping back, paunch jiggling as he danced with marvelous speed. Shift and flash went the axe, and shift and flash again, moving with the speed and control of a light sword, though the heaviest sword could not have held it in a parry. A light murmur of awe went around the watching circle.

Sosias tried the cut at the thighs again, or feinted doing so. This time the riposte came out a little farther after him, yet he miraculously managed to cut his own movement short at the critical instant and slide away untouched. His concealed knife had come out into his left hand, but he was unable now to get close enough to use it.

It would be suicidal to simply wait and try to keep dodging that axe. Sosias must try to attack again, and at last the great axe caught him coming in, and wiped away his face. Thomas the Grabber, leaning on his spear some ten meters distant, felt warm droplets of blood splash on his arm.

"Thomas the Grabber—Vann the Nomad."

Vann with his clumsy-looking grip on his long sword faced Thomas, who probingly sent his huge spear darting out and back. Vann wasted no energy in trying to behead the spear, the armored shaft of which had proved itself already in several fights. The fight developed quite slowly at first, both men moving cautiously, with many feints and no real effort at attack.

After a while it became apparent to expert eyes—no other kind were watching now—that

Vann could not entirely rid himself of the affectation of holding his sword awkwardly between exchanges. Certainly he got it back into the proper position with amazing speed, but the fraction of a heartbeat wasted in this correction was more than could be spared in competition at this level. The awkward grip was not a natural attitude for Vann, like Kelsumba's peculiar way of holding his axe, but a pose practiced to put an opponent off guard. As such it was utterly useless now, as Vann knew full well; he did not want to use it, but his nerves and muscles would forget and fall into the pattern.

Thomas timed this lapse and recovery several times, then caught the long sword drooping on the downbeat. With a sound like a club's impact the spear rammed through Vann's tattered shirt and torso, a little above his trophied belt. Vann's face bore a look of witless grief when he saw the bright fountain of his own blood, then bore no expression at all.

Farley of Eikosk, departing from that deadly ring in the company of his three peers, to resume their slow trek up the mountain, was bothered by the eerie feeling that the gods had forgotten the surviving handful of them. Glancing back over his shoulder from the next bend in the road, he saw the stiffening bodies of the day's four victims laid out beside the ring, and a single gray-garbed figure with a maul at its belt beginning to dig the modest pit that would be their grave. Isaksson, walking beside Farley, kept glancing back also, and Isaksson, too, seemed perturbed

about something. Farley almost tried to speak of
his troubled feelings, but then said nothing,
being unsure of how to put them into words.

A few paces ahead, Omir Kelsumba, his huge
axe clean and sheathed and innocent as some
woodcutter's implement, went up the endless-
seeming hill with easy strides. His thoughts were
far away, with his small unhealthy children and
his wife. Someday, if he won the Tournament, he
could perhaps return to see his family, drifting as
a spirit on the night wind, or coming with
changed appearance as a casual traveler. Everyone knew that gods could do such things, and
when he had won the Tournament he would be
almost a god.

Earlier there had been occasional doubts, but
now the conviction had returned that he was
going to win. He waxed stronger with every victory. He could feel the god-strength mounting in
him. Since he had reached his full growth, no
man had ever been able to stand against him,
and none could now. When the Tournament was
over he would be a god, and gods could heal as
well as murder. When he took his seat at
Thorun's right hand the goddess of healing
could not refuse to grant him healing for his children. No child of a god was ever done to death in
a hovel by ill luck or mean diseases.

Walking beside Omir Kelsumba, but guessing
nothing of his thoughts, Thomas the Grabber
went up with him stride for stride. Despite a lifetime of violence as bandit, soldier, bodyguard,
and bounty hunter of dangerous men, Thomas

still fell from time to time into the grip of an almost paralyzing fear of bodily injury and death. Iron control was needed to keep his fear from showing. The fear was on him now, and a premonition that he must lose in his next fight. There was nothing in sight for him beyond the wide blade of Kelsumba's axe, at which he dared not look. Thomas was experienced enough with this kind of fear to know that it would pass if only he could manage to hold out against it until he had actually entered the ring with his opponent. Then things would be all right, there would be no time for fear. No one could stand against him then. Now as he climbed he held on grimly to his nerve, trying to think of nothing.

The road came to the twin towers from which sentinels saluted gravely as the fighters passed.

"The gods' private park," Thomas muttered aloud, looking around him as they continued. The road was wider now, bordered with fine gravel walks, beyond which cultivated green ground-cover vines made one continuously inviting couch.

"Yes," said Farley of Eikosk's reverent voice behind him. "I suppose we might see Thorun himself among those trees."

No one answered. Shortly Yelgir, their escorting priest, signalled for a halt, and led them a little distance off the road. The ground was softer than before, its area smaller. The night was quiet when it came, still as the grave, or nearly so.

IX

Schoenberg, De La Torre, Athena, and Celeste were returned to their comfortable private rooms after the feast, but they were kept under guard every step of the way and all pretense that they were free agents had been dropped. No one was manhandled, but all were searched and their communicators taken from them.

None would speak to them; Andreas had left and no one else was willing to answer their protests and questions.

While they were being led from the Temple back to their rooms there was time to exchange a few words. Schoenberg advised his shipmates: "Whatever it is they want, they'll tell us when they're ready. Meanwhile it's important that we all keep our heads."

"We'll back you up, Oscar," Athena told him. Behind her determined face, those of Celeste and De La Torre were pale and frightened.

Schoenberg winked at her. Then they were put firmly into their separate rooms. He could hear his door being locked and barred. His personal servant had disappeared and when he peered out through the grillwork of the window he saw that a guard had been stationed outside his door. Schoenberg stretched out on the comfortable bed and tried to think. After a while he got up and tried tapping messages on the stone wall between his room and Athena's, but there was no reply. Probably the masonry was too thick.

Surprisingly, he slept well and felt reasonably rested when he was awakened early in the morning. An escort of soldiers had come to take him to Andreas. He went with them eagerly. They re-entered the Temple by another of its back doors and again went down some steps, this time to a cell-like stone chamber into which gray morning light filtered through a single high window. Andreas was seated behind a table. Schoenberg's escort saluted and went out; he and the ancient and ugly High Priest were left alone. Andreas was the thinner of the two, and biologically much the older, but he wore a dagger at the girdle of his purplish robe, and seemed utterly unconcerned about being left alone with a bigger and stronger man who had just become his enemy.

Even before the door had closed behind the soldiers, Schoenberg spoke. "If you are wise, Andreas, you will free us at once."

Andreas calmly gestured to a chair, but Schoenberg remained standing. The High Priest then said: "Before I can dismiss your guards I must have assurance that you are going to cooperate in the project in which we are going to use your ship. Your willing cooperation will be a great help, though not essential."

"Imprisoning me and my friends does not make me want to cooperate. What about the other two members of my party—what has happened to them?"

Andreas folded his hands on the table before him. "The girl is confined to her stateroom on your ship. She is there to speak reassuringly over ships' radio, on the remote chance that another spaceship should appear and attempt to contact the *Orion*."

"Last night your people threatened her, frightened her, so that when she spoke to me she dared not tell me what had happened."

"She has seen the wisdom of cooperation." Andreas spoke mildly. "As for the coward, he is still missing. Probably he will come to no great harm, and will be back looking for food today or tomorrow. I am not going to demean my warriors by ordering them to search for him."

After a moment's silence Schoenberg took the chair that had been offered to him earlier. "What exactly do you want me to do?"

"Answer some questions about your ship, its drive in particular, and move the ship for us when the time comes."

There was a little pause. "You will have to tell me more than that. I do not want to get into serious trouble with the outworld authorities."

The High Priest shook his head. "Right now I am the only authority with whom you must concern yourself. Those outside this planet may be powerful in their own worlds, but they would not care much what happens here, even if they could know."

Schoenberg relaxed a trifle, crossed one leg
over the other. "That is half true, Andreas. They
do not care about such hunting trips as mine,
not really. Not enough to take the time and trouble to prevent them. They would not care much
about my standing and watching your Tournament—or even taking part in it, if I could have
been so honored. But they will care, believe me,
if I should take part in one of your wars, using
outworld weapons, or even using the ship to help
you in any military way. Doing any such thing
would be a grave risk for me; not a battlerisk,
understand, which a man should welcome, but a
social risk when I have returned to my own people, a risk of dishonor. Being an honorable man
yourself, you will appreciate why I cannot help
you."

"I assure you most solemnly, no one outside
this planet will ever know what you do here."

"Excuse me, but I doubt that. I am not the
only hunter to come to this planet, and sooner or
later a trader or a military ship will call. Your
enemies on this planet cannot be entirely silenced, and they will not miss the chance to com-
plain about the spaceship that, unprovoked,
molested them, and it will be discovered that the
ship was mine. I mention these facts first, because you may not believe me when I tell you
that, in any case, the Earth authorities will be
concerned if I fail to return from this trip on
time." Schoenberg lifted his arm casually and
briefly glanced at his calendar watch.

Andreas smiled slightly. "No one on Earth or
any of the other worlds knows where you are.

Whatever search is made for you will not be on my planet."

Schoenberg did not hesitate for a moment. So far he had not shown the slightest sign of fear. "It will be your mistake, High Priest, if you do not believe me. But never mind that now. Let us return to what you want. Say that I am now sitting in the command chair in the control room of my ship with you presumably leaning over me and holding a knife against my throat. Where to?"

"Schoenberg, I am not literally going to hold a knife against your throat. Not in your control room anyway, where you might be tempted to push something the wrong way in an effort to disrupt my plans. There is a priest here who has been aboard spaceships before, and we are not so utterly ignorant of them as you might suppose . . . I had thought you might be willing to join in a military sort of adventure. De La Torre would be, but he is ignorant. I have questioned the other people of your party, and believe them when they say they know nothing about the ship's drive, nor of pilotage."

"That is correct. I am the only pilot here."

"Tell me, for my curiosity, how could they have gotten home if a glacier-beast had killed you?"

"Autopilot could handle that. Just punch in a destination, and it'll deliver you in-system, near any civilized world you want. Your priest who's been aboard spaceships must know that. I take it you want some other kind of piloting."

"Yes. But mainly some detailed information about the drive."

"Tell me what it's all about and maybe I'll provide that information."

Andreas's eyes probed at him, not fiercely but deeply, for what seemed a long time. "Perhaps that would be best." The old priest sighed. "Perhaps other ways . . . tell me, what effect do threats of torture and maiming have upon you?"

Schoenberg half rose, and leaned forward glaring. "High Priest, I am a powerful man out there, in the big world that holds your little world surrounded. Do you think that just anyone can possess his own starship and take it where he likes? I have made it in the interest of several other powerful and ruthless people to look out for my safety, to avenge my death or disappearance. And those people *do* know exactly where I am and when I am due to return. For every dol of pain you make me suffer, you will feel two, or perhaps ten, of one kind of pain or another. My friends and I can pull down your city and your Temple if you provoke us to it. Now threaten me no more!"

The two men's eyes were still locked when there came a tap at the door and it opened and one of the Inner Circle put in his head, making a slight nodding signal to Andreas. Other business called.

The High Priest sighed and arose. Smiling, skull-faced, he bowed his head very slightly in salute to Schoenberg. "You are a hard man to frighten, outworlder. Nevertheless I think it will be worthwhile to do so. Think for a while on what I have said, and shortly we will talk again."

* * *

Suomi was afraid.

He was not simply afraid of being caught by Andreas's soldiers, who yesterday had taken the ship and Barbara and had no doubt also swept up the four other unsuspecting outworlders with little difficulty. No, the night in the thicket had given Suomi plenty of time to think and there was a lot more to it than that.

Hours ago he had left the thicket where yesterday his flight had come to an exhausted halt. Now he was crouched in the poor concealment of some thin, bush-like vegetation near the road that climbed the mountain, watching and waiting—for what he was not exactly sure. He had vague hopes of spying some lone traveler whom he might approach in hopes of getting some kind of help.

Alternatively he imagined another pack train of the kind he had already seen, passing by, and a convenient bag of vegetables or haunch of meat tumbling forgotten to the road, where he might spring out a minute later to grab it up. He had as yet found nothing very palatable in the woods and thickets, and so he had not eaten anything worth mentioning in more than a standard day.

He was also thirsty, despite the rainwater he had licked from some dripping leaves, and he was limping fairly badly from yesterday's fall. His back bothered him, and he thought that one of the minor cuts on his leg might be infected, despite the routine immunological precautions taken before leaving Earth.

The thicket into which he had burrowed himself when he stopped running was so dense and extensive that it seemed possible that a man might stay there undiscovered—until it pleased his pursuers to detail a hundred men or so to hunt him out. But perhaps Suomi had no pursuers. On this alien planet he had literally nowhere to go. He suspected strongly that his continued freedom, if it could be called that, was due only to the fact that no particular effort had been made to round him up. He could not believe that the warriors of Hunters' were particularly afraid of dying by his rifle, so it must be that they were not hunting him because more important things were going on.

Realizing that he could not accomplish anything there he had left the thicket. There was a warning to be spread. At moments it seemed possible that the whole thing had been no more than a monstrous practical joke, like an initiation . . . but then he recalled his dark clear thoughts of the night just past, and shivered a little in the warmth of day. It was not only for himself that he feared, and not only for the people who had come with him from Earth. In his mind's eye Suomi could still see with perfect clarity the robot's shattered carapace, the debris of components spilling out. And there, mixed with all the handmade parts . . .

"Softly, outworlder," said a gentle voice quite close behind him.

He whirled and found he was presenting the rifle at a rather short man with sandy hair, who was standing beside a tree six or eight meters off, muscular arms raised and hands open in an unmistakable gesture of peace. The man wore

the gray clothing Suomi had seen on
Godsmountain's slaves, and tucked into the
heavy rope that served him as a belt was a short
massive sledge. The killer of fallen gladiators.
The man stood taller than Suomi remembered
and also had a more open and attractive face.

"What do you want?" Suomi held the rifle
steady, though his gaze went darting around the
woods. No one else was in sight; the slave had
come here alone.

"Only to talk with you a little." The man's
tone was reassuring. He very slowly lowered his
hands but otherwise did not move. "To make
common cause with you, if I can, against our
common enemies." He nodded in an uphill direction.

Did slaves on Hunters' habitually talk like
this? Suomi doubted it. He scarcely remembered
hearing them talk at all. He did not relax. "How
did you find me?"

"I guessed you might be somewhere near the
road by this time, thinking about giving up. I
have been trying to find you for an hour, and I
doubt anyone else has made the effort."

Suomi nodded. "I guessed that much. Who
are you? Not a slave."

"You are right. I am not. But more of that
later. Come, move back into the woods, before
someone sees us from the road."

Now Suomi did relax, lowering the rifle with
shaking hands and following the other back into
the trees, where they squatted down to talk.

"First, tell me this," the man demanded at once.
"How can we prevent Andreas and his band of
thieves from making use of your stolen ship?"

"I don't know. Where are my companions?"

"Held in the Temple, under what conditions I am not sure. You don't look good. I would offer you food and drink, but have none with me at the moment. Why do you think Andreas wants your ship?"

"I am afraid." Suomi shook his head. "If it is only Andreas I suppose he has some simple military use in mind to complete his conquest of this planet. He may think our ship carries weapons of mass destruction. It has none."

The man was looking sharply at Suomi. "What did you mean, if it is only Andreas?"

"Have you heard of the berserkers?"

A blank look. "Of course, the death machines of legend. What have they to do with this?"

Suomi began to describe his combat with the man-shaped machine. His hearer was ready to listen.

"I heard a rumor that Mjollnir had walked forth to fight, and was slain," the man in gray mused. "So, it was a berserker that you destroyed?"

"Not exactly. Not entirely. Against a true berserker android this rifle would have been useless. But inside the machine's broken body I found this." He drew from his pocket a small sealed box of shiny metal. From the box a thick gray cable emerged, to expand into a fan of innumerable gauze-fine fibers at the point where his force packet had sheared it off. "This is a solid-state electronuclear device, in other words part of an artificial brain. Judging from its size, and the number of fibers in this cable, I would

say that two or three of these, properly intercon-
nected, should be enough to control a robot that
could do physical things better than a man can
do them, and also obey simple orders and make
simple decisions."

The man reached for the box and weighed it
doubtfully in his hand.

Suomi went on: "Many solid-state electronuclear devices are made on Earth and other
technological worlds. I have seen countless varie-
ties of them. Do you know how many I have seen
that closely resemble this? Exactly one. I saw
that in a museum. It was part of a berserker,
captured in a space battle at the Stone Place,
long ago."

The man scratched his chin, and handed back
the box. "It is hard for me to take a legend as
reality."

Suomi felt like grabbing him and shaking him.
"Berserkers are very real, I promise you. What
do you suppose destroyed the technology of your
forefathers, here on Hunters'?"

"We are taught as children that our ancestors
were too proud and strong to let themselves remain dependent on fancy machines. Oh, the legends tell of a war against berserkers, too."

"It is not only legend but history."

"All right, history. What is your point?"

"That war cut off your ancestors from the rest
of the galaxy for a long time and wrecked their
technology—as you say, they were rough men
and women who found they could get by without
a lot of fancy machines. Made a virtue of necessi-
ty. Anyway, it has been taken for granted that
Karlsen's victory here destroyed all the

berserkers on Hunters' or drove them away. But
perhaps one survived, or at least its unliving
brain survived when the rest of its machinery
was crippled or destroyed. Perhaps that
berserker is still here."

His auditor was still receptive but unimpressed. Suomi decided that more explanation
was in order. He went on: "On other planets
there have been cults of evil men and women
who have worshipped berserkers as gods. I can
only guess that there might have been some such
people on Hunters' five hundred years ago. After
the battle they found their crippled god somewhere, rescued it and hid it. Built a secret cult
around it, worshipped it in secret, generation after generation. Praying to Death, working for the
day when they could destroy all life upon this
planet."

The man ran strong-looking, nervous fingers
through his sandy hair. "But, if you are right,
there was more to it than the figure of Mjollnir?
The berserker has not been destroyed?"

"I am sure there is more to it than that. The
real berserker brain must have included many
more of these small units. And other components
as well. Probably it put only spare parts into
Mjollnir. Or human artisans did, working at the
berserker's direction."

"Then why must there be a true berserker, as
you put it, here at all? Andreas has very good
artisans working for him. Perhaps they only used
parts from destroyed berserkers to build the figure of Mjollnir—and one of Thorun as well." He
nodded to himself. "That would explain why

men swear they have actually seen Thorun walking with the High Priest in the Temple courtyards."

"Excuse me, but it is not possible that any human artisans on this planet designed the robot that attacked me. No matter what components they had to work with. Can you grasp the programming problems involved in designing a machine to run and fight and climb like a man? Better than a man. No human could have climbed that mesa where the machine did it, in a few minutes, hammering in pitons all the way. And the mechanical engineering difficulties? No. On Earth, Venus, a handful of other planets, there are men and facilities capable of designing such a robot. Only a functioning berserker-brain could do it here."

The two men were quiet for a little while, both thinking, each studying the other. Suomi eased himself into a different position, sitting with his back against a tree trunk. His wounded leg throbbed. At last the Hunterian said: "Suppose a berserker is here as you say, and the priests of Godsmountain have it. What then?"

"You do not understand!" Suomi almost grabbed him by the ragged shirt to attempt a shaking. "Say rather that it has them. How can I begin to tell you what a berserker is?" He sighed and slumped back, feeling hopeless and exhausted. How to convey, to someone who had never seen even depictions on film or holograph, the centuries of mass destruction berserkers had visited upon the galaxy, the documented cases of

individual horrors? Whole planets had been ster-
ilized, whole solar systems laid waste by the unliving enemy. People by the thousands or tens of
thousands had perished in berserkers' experi-
ments aimed at discovering what made the
strange two-legged Earth-descended blobs of
protoplasm so resistant to the fundamental
truth-assumption of the berserkers' programming: that life was a disease of matter that had
to be expunged. It had all happened here, was
still happening somewhere a thousand light
years or more away, on the outer edge of man's
little domain within the galaxy.

Suomi said quietly: "If it is true that a
berserker has captured our ship then it can be
for only one purpose; to somehow sterilize this
planet of all life."

"You said there were no mass weapons on the
ship!"

"I meant there were none in the usual sense.
But there is the drive that brought us between
the stars." Suomi considered. "If the ship were
buried beneath this mountain, say, and the drive
suddenly turned on full force, the mountain
might be blown up into the air and everyone on
it killed. Not good enough for a berserker, not if
it could find a way of doing worse.

"I'll bet that if the drive were worked on cun-
ningly enough some weapon could be made of it
that could sterilize a planet. Perhaps by pollut-
ing the atmosphere with radioactivity. The
weapon wouldn't have to be instantly effective.
There probably won't be another interstellar
ship here for fifteen standard years. No way for

anyone here to call for outside help, even if they understood what was happening."

The man in gray was excited at last. He stood up cautiously and looked about, then squatted down again. He fingered the handle of his maul, as if itching to pull it from his belt and fight. "By all the gods!" he muttered. "It should be effective, whether or not it is the truth!"

"Effective? What should be?"

"It should be effective against Godsmountain's priests, to spread the story that the drive of the captured ship is to be altered, our air poisoned. That a berserker really rules Godsmountain, and means to destroy the world. If we can convince people of that, we will have them!"

"It is the truth, I believe. But to spread any story across the planet will take far too long."

The man with the maul glanced up toward the mountaintop, invisible beyond the trees. "I do not think we will need to go that far. Now. How to put the story in convincing terms? Let's see. Five hundred standard years ago the berserker fleet was here. The demigod Karlsen drove them out. The priests for some reason have been asking if any of your outworlders mentioned Karlsen; that seems to fit. Now—"

Now Suomi did actually seize him by the shirt, to the Hunterian's great astonishment. "They asked that?" Suomi barked. "Of course it fits!"

For half an hour thereafter they made their plans.

X

The four remaining contestants were awakened early from their sleep on the soft groundcover of what Thomas the Grabber had called the gods' private park. At dawn there erupted a racket of small winged creatures, each defending his bit of territory against encroachment by the others. Farley of Eikosk, roused by the noise of this miniature Tournament, watched it for a while, and then, with sudden awareness of where he was, turned his gaze uphill through the park-like forest, toward the summit of the mountain.

There, in the early morning light, the white walls had a dull and ghostly look. Later, he knew, when he saw them in full sunlight, they would shine a dazzling white. All his life he had listened eagerly, whenever he could, to the tales of travelers who had visited this city. To see its white stones actually before him inspired him with awe.

Thorun lived there.

Thorun actually lived there.

From the moment of Farley's awakening on

this morning a sense of unreality grew in him
rapidly. He could not fully credit his own presence here on the mountaintop, or his success
thus far in the Tournament. (How pleased his
father would be, at last, if he should be the winner!) This feeling of unreality persisted through
the morning ritual of worship, and through their
meager breakfast of cold fried cakes left over
from the day before. The dumb slave who served
them protested with gestures that no dead wood
was available here to make a fire for cooking.

The other slave had gone off somewhere, perhaps on a search for wood. Leros still had not
returned. The priest Yelgir, who still seemed a
stranger to Farley, looked stiff-jointed and di-
sheveled after a night spent in the open. He
spoke to them apologetically about the fact that
no fighting ring had been prepared here in advance.

Yelgir, in consultation with the warriors,
chose a flat area of ground and the slave was set
to work stripping away the groundcover and
stamping flat the earth as best he could. The
task took the slave several hours, while the others
sat watching.

Farley was not exactly impatient, but the delay was one more change in routine, and made
everything all the more unreal for him. At last
the ring was ready, however. Yelgir was mutter-
ing prayers and it was time for the first two men
to fight to take their places.

"Farley of Eikosk—Jud Isaksson."

Now both of them were in the circle from
which only one of them could ever walk. But as

Jud moved toward him, more slowly than was his wont, it occurred to Farley that death itself might well be different here, almost under the windows of Thorun's hall. Would the loser of this fight really die as men usually did, like some butchered animal? Might he not instead simply look down at his gaping wound, acknowledge defeat with a salute and a courteous nod, and, like one leaving a field of harmless practice, simply walk off yonder through the trees, perhaps to be met halfway by welcoming Mjollnir or Karlsen or even Thorun himself?

In Farley's eyes the scimitar flashed sunlight. Jud was warming up now, starting to come on with his usual fury. Farley suddenly felt free and loose, faster and stronger than ever in his life before. It was as if he now breathed in the immortality of the gods by merely sharing their high air.

He parried the scimitar with a seeming carelessness that was really something else, and then he stepped in looking for the best way to kill. Now Farley carried his long sword too high, now too low, now he let his blade stray far aside into what should have been a weak position, until he could almost hear his father shouting at him in anger, but none of this was carelessness. Not today. Whatever tactic his whims, his nerves, chose for him was fated to succeed. His blade always came back into position in time to block the scimitar. On the attack his long sword reached closer and closer to Jud's lifeblood.

To Farley the end seemed foreordained and only the suddenness with which it came sur-

prised him. He stood there almost disappointed
that the fight was over, while Jud dying on the
ground seemed to be trying to tell him something. Jud's life ran out too quickly, before the
words could come.

The priest Yelgir cleared his throat. "Omir
Kelsumba—Thomas the Grabber." Today he
needed no paper to keep track of names.

Standing to one side, Farley was struck by the
realization that in this round, for the first time,
there would be no other victors to stand at his
side watching with him, now and then passing a
joke or a comment on the fight in progress.
Watching alone, except for the priest, he beheld
a serene happiness on Kelsumba's face; obviously here was another who felt favored by the gods
today. Things appeared to be different with
Thomas the Grabber. Even before the first blow
his expression was that of a man who knows
himself defeated.

In the center of the ring the two of them closed
promptly. The axe flashed out with reckless confidence with what must be Kelsumba's certainty
of approaching godhood. The spear moved with
the speed of desperation, and yet as accurately
and steadily as if wielded by a god. Incredibly,
the fight was over.

Or was it over? Kelsumba, even with the
heavy spear transfixing him, fought on. His axe,
though it was much slower now, still rose and
fell. Thomas was still unhurt. But instead of
backing away and waiting for his man to fall, he
chose for some reason to leap in and grab. As the
two men wrestled it was still Omir who smiled,

and Thomas who looked desperate. But it was quickly demonstrated that Omir was not the stronger of the two, at least not with a spear stuck through him. Only after Thomas had wrenched away the axe and used it for a finishing blow did his face lose its look of desperation.

Now the clangor of arms, that had long since silenced the winged quarreling creatures, was ended also. The forest at last was still.

When Schoenberg was brought before him again, about midday, Andreas was seated as before. As soon as the two of them were left alone, the High Priest began: "Since the thought of torture does not immediately terrify you, and I suspect its application might provoke you to some rash attempt at misinforming us about the ship, I have decided I must take an extreme measure to frighten you sufficiently. You have brought it on yourself." Andreas was smiling again, evidently finding his own wit amusing.

Schoenberg, unimpressed, sat down. "How do you mean to terrify me, then?" he answered.

"By saying a few words."

"Andreas, my respect for you is fading. If the threats you have already made have not had their desired effect neither will any mutterings about some great unnameable terror. You are not going to scare me that way. In fact you are not going to scare me at all, not in the way you seem to want."

"I think I can. I think I know what a man like you is truly afraid of."

"What?"

"Perhaps I can do it by saying to you only one word." Andreas clapped his hands together playfully.

Schoenberg waited.

"The one word is his name."

"Thorun. I know that."

"No. Thorun is a toy. My god is real."

"Well, then. Utter this terrible name." Schoenberg lifted his eyebrows in almost jaunty inquiry.

Andreas whispered the three syllables.

It took Schoenberg a little while to grasp it. At first he was merely puzzled. "Berserker," he repeated, leaning back in his chair, his face a blank.

Andreas waited, confidently, for his god had never failed him yet.

Schoenberg said: "You mean . . . ahhh. I think I begin to see. You mean one has really been here for five hundred years, and you—serve it?"

"I am going shortly to offer to the god of Death a special sacrifice, consisting of some people we no longer need. I can show you. You will be convinced."

"Yes, I believe you can show me. I believe you. Well. This puts a different face on things, all right, but not in the way you intended. If I wouldn't help you in a local war, I'm not going to help you in a mass extermination."

"Schoenberg, when we have done with this planet what we will, when it is moribund, my god assures me that the ship's drive can be restored sufficiently to take it out into space again and after a voyage of many years to reach another star whose planets also are polluted by the foul scum of life. I and a few others, members of my Inner Circle, will make this voyage, continuing to bear the burden of hideous life on our own bodies that we may free many others of it on other worlds. There are emergency recycling systems on your ship that will nourish us adequately for years.

"The voyage, as I have said, will be many years in duration. Unless you agree to cooperate with me from this moment on you will be brought with us as a prisoner. You will not die. There are ways of preventing suicide, my master assures me, things he can do to your brain when he has time to work on it.

"You will be useful on the voyage, for we will have need of a servant. You will not be tortured —I mean, not much at any one time. I will see to it that your sufferings never become sharp enough to set one day of your existence apart from another. I may die before the voyage is over, but some of my associates are young men and they will follow my orders faithfully. You Earthmen are very long-lived, I understand. I suppose you will—what did the old Earthmen call it?—go mad. No one will ever admire your exploits. There will be none to admire. But I suppose you might continue to exist to an age of five hundred years."

Schoenberg had not moved. Now a muscle twitched in his right cheek. His head had bowed a very little, his shoulders were a little lower than before.

Andreas said: "I would much prefer to see you make a sporting finish, myself. Go out with a noble gesture. If you cooperate in my plans, a different future for you might be arranged. You will only be helping us to do what we are going to do anyway.

"If you cooperate, I will give you"—Andreas held up a hand, thumb and forefinger barely separated—"just a *little* chance, at the very end. You will not win, but you will die nobly in the attempt."

"What kind of chance?" Schoenberg's voice was low and desperate now. He blinked repeatedly.

"Give you a sword, let you try to hack your way past one of my fighting men, to get to the berserker and cut it into bits. Its cabling would be quite vulnerable to such an attack."

"You wouldn't really do that! It is your god."

Andreas waited calmly.

"How do I know that you would really do that?" The words burst out as if involuntarily.

"You know now what I will do if you do not cooperate."

The silence in the little room stretched on and on.

Only three men, not counting a slave or two, now remained on their feet under the pleasant trees of the gods' otherwise deserted park. Farley and Thomas stood facing each other, their eyes meeting like those of two strangers encountering each other by chance in a wilderness both had thought uninhabited. In the background the

priest was giving orders to the slaves; there was
the chunk of a shovel starting a new grave.

Farley looked down at what lay on the
ground. Jud had not smiled at his wound and
gone off on a blithe stroll among the trees.
Kelsumba was not laughing on his way to an
eternal feast with gods. Farley did not care to
stay and watch them rolled into a little pit. Feeling a slow emergence from his sensation of in-
vulnerability, he turned and started on the uphill
road once more.

Thomas the Grabber, still wiping at his spear,
came along silently and companionably. They
left the priest behind. Here the pavement of the
road was very smooth and well maintained, and
it was neatly bordered with stones in a pattern
that put Farley in mind of certain formal walks
on his father's large estate.

Now, with what seemed to Farley stunning or-
dinariness, they were coming through the last
trees of the forest and around the road's last
curve. Vistas opened, and gardens and orchards
were visible in the distance to either side. Ahead,
the road ran straight across thirty or forty meters
of well-tended lawn, and then it entered the
citadel-city of the gods. The gate by which it entered, of massive timbers banded with wrought
metal, was tightly closed just now. The high wall
of the city was a blinding white in the sun, and
Farley was now close enough to see how huge
and heavy its stones were. He wondered how
they had been stained or painted to make them
look like bone.

But nothing happened inside him when he

beheld their goal, the place where Thorun dwelled. Immortality was draining from him rapidly.

"Thomas," he said, slowing to a halt. "The whole thing is too—ordinary."

"How's that?" asked Thomas, amiably, stopping at his side.

Farley paused. How to explain his disappointment? He could not understand it well himself. He said what came to his tongue, which was only: "There were sixty-four of us, and now there are only two."

"But how else could it have worked out?" Thomas asked reasonably.

A few weeds grew through the rocks beside Thorun's gateway. Lumps of the dried dung of some pack animal lay at the roadside. Farley threw back his head and closed his eyes. He groaned.

"What is it, friend?"

"Thomas, Thomas. What do you see here, what do you feel? Suddenly I am having doubts." He looked at his companion for help.

Thomas shook his head. "Oh my friend, there is no doubt at all about our future. You and I are going to fight, and then only one of us is going living through that gate."

There was the gate, tough ordinary wood, bound with bands of wrought metal, its lower parts showing a little superficial wear from the brushing passages of countless men and women, slaves and animals. Behind such a gate there could be nothing but more of the same world in which Farley now stood, in which he had lived all his life. And if he reached the gate of the Temple inside, would it be any different?

The priest Yelgir, whom they had left behind, came on now to pass them, giving Farley an uneasy smile as he did so. Evidently some unseen watcher within the walls noted the priest's approach, for now the gate was opened slightly from within. Another priest stuck out his head and sized up Farley and Thomas with an impersonal look. "Is either of them wounded?" he asked Yelgir.

"One has a damaged hand, and cannot use his dagger, but that seems to bother him very little. The other a sliced arm. The muscle is not cut, nothing serious." The two priests began a low-voiced conversation that Farley could not quite hear. Meanwhile other heads, obviously aristocratic, began to appear along the top of the wall, their owners evidently standing on some high walkway on the inner side. The two finalists of Thorun's Tournament were being stared at like slaves on auction. Thomas the Grabber finished wiping his spear and now stood leaning on it, shifting his weight from one foot to the other and sighing.

"Bid the two contestants wait," someone was calling carelessly from inside. "The High Pirest sends word that he hopes to attend the final duel, but he is busy now with some special sacrifice to the gods."

XI

Suomi, after his talk with the man in gray (whose name he had never learned), breathed a sigh of relief mingled with exhaustion when he had gotten as far as the foot of the little mesa without being discovered and seized by Andreas's men. Suomi had to somehow manage to get himself into the ship again, before he could hope to accomplish anything. He must not be captured before he reached the mesa.

According to the gauge on the breech of his rifle, it had power left for only six shots. He might have thrown away the weapon in the woods, except for his fear that some fool might find it and kill himself or someone else by accident. He had offered the rifle to the man in gray, when they were about to part, but the offer was refused.

"I must continue to pass as a slave," the Hunterian had said. "No slave could carry such a device into the city without immediately being questioned. Besides, I am unfamiliar with its use; better each man to his own weapons."

"Each to his own," Suomi had answered,

reaching out for a farewell handshake. "Good
luck with yours. I hope I meet you in the city
above."

Now, at the foot of the mesa, he observed that
a regular trail had already been worn, leading
from the lower end of the climbing path off into
the woods uphill in the direction of the city. He
observed also that not a trace remained of the
shattered robot; at first he could not even locate
the place where it had lain. Then he realized
that the massive tree, whose surface his rifle fire
had splintered, had been removed. Here was the
neatly sawn stump, with dirt rubbed on the cut
surface so it would not look fresh. The tree itself
had somehow been carried away. Great pains
were being taken to eliminate all evidence that
anything grotesque had happened here. But a
number of men must have been involved in the
cleanup and at least one of them must have
talked, so the man in gray had rumors to build
on. So much the better.

When he got to the bottom of the climbing
path, Suomi did shrug out of the rifle's strap and
let the weapon fall aside. Gratefully he saw that
the climbing rope was still in place. Fighting
down a foolish impulse to turn at the last moment and run away to cower in the woods once
more, he gritted his teeth and gripped the rope
and began to climb. Weakened and aching, he
was now compelled to hang on with both hands
even on the easy first part of the slope, where
before he had been able to climb rapidly on legs
alone.

He had gotten only a little way up when a sol-

dier came into view, looked down and saw
Suomi, and began shouting. Suomi ignored the
shouts and continued to struggle slowly upward.
The shouting kept on. Suomi looked up and saw
that the man had a spear raised as if ready to
throw.

"If you stick me with that thing," Suomi
yelled back at last, "you'll have to carry me.
Look at me. Am I so dangerous that I frighten
you?"

His belly muscles were tensing against the impact of the spear, but it did not come. The voice
stopped shouting, moved away just a little, and
began to talk. Other male voices answered.
Suomi did not pay much attention to what they
were saying, and did not look up again. Dizzy
with hunger and fatigue, feverish from his infected wound, he struggled on the rocks for what
seemed an endless time before he could pull himself out on the flat horizontal surface at the head
of the path.

The foam mattress lay almost under his feet
when he stood up but there was no sign of
Barbara. Half a dozen men, four soldiers and
two priests in purple-trimmed robes, crowded
around Suomi, barking threats and orders at
him, almost nudging him off the mesa again with
their drawn swords and a leveled spear. Finally
one of the aristocrats raised his voice and there
was order. The soldiers put down their weapons,
rapidly stripped Suomi and searched him, then
searched through his clothes and tossed them
back to him.

"What've you done with the girl who was

here?" he asked while this was going on. No one bothered to answer.

"Bring him inside the ship," one of the aristocrats ordered the soldiers.

"We'd better get on the communicator first and ask Andreas," the other one advised. After a moment's debate they compromised and had Suomi brought up the landing ramp as far as the open entrance lock. There they left him standing for the moment, with two soldiers gripping his arms. His guards were unusually large, strong men, and once the initial confusion of his capture was over they obeyed orders with precision and alertness.

Suomi wished he could sit down, but was not quite certain that he would be able to get up again if he did. He could hear voices from the direction of the control room engaged in what sounded like a talk on the communicator between the ship and somewhere else. Andreas's prize-crew perhaps had more technological savvy than Suomi had assumed. So much the worse.

In a little while one of the aristocrats came back from the direction of the control room to stand in front of Suomi and regard him critically. "Andreas is busy with sacrifice. I think we'll just bring this one on board, and confine him to his old stateroom. The place has been searched a dozen times, there are no weapons. Outworlder, you look in a bad way."

"If I could have some food . . ."

"We won't starve you to death, I don't suppose. Though you may wish we had." He signed to the soldiers to bring Suomi on into the ship.

At the entrance to the control room the aristocrat turned. "Hold him tightly going through here."

They brought him into the control room, and they were quite right to make sure that he was held securely. Otherwise it might have been barely possible for him to lunge at the drive controls and, before he could be stopped, wreck the ship. But there was no hope of that, his arms were pinned in grips he could not have broken on his strongest days, of which this was not one.

Seated in the large central pilot's chair was another aristocratic priest.

On a screen before him were the faces of two men who seemed to be in some dimly lighted stone chamber. The one in the background was another priest. The one in front was Schoenberg.

"Now," the priest in the control chair was saying, addressing the screen, "you say that if the ship pitches more than ten degrees while under manual control, the autopilot will cut in automatically?"

"Yes," Schoenberg's image said on the screen. "Provided the artificial gravity is off. The ten degrees pitch and you'll get the autopilot."

"Schoenberg!" Suomi cried out. "Don't fly it for them, Schoenberg, it's a berserker they're working for. Don't do anything they want!"

Schoenberg's face showed a reaction, though only a trivial one, and his eyes moved, probably following Suomi's passage through the control room on a portable screen taken from the ship. The men transporting Suomi were making no particular effort to hush him up or hurry him along.

"A berserker, Schoenberg!"

Schoenberg's eyes on the screen closed. His face looked deathly tired. His voice came wearily into the ship. "I know what I'm doing, Suomi. Just go along with them. Don't make things more difficult than they are."

Suomi with his escort passed out of the control room and into the narrow passage leading to the staterooms, moving at a brisk pace. The doors of most of the rooms and compartments stood open, revealing scenes of disorder, but that of the room that had been Barbara's was closed. A bored-looking soldier stood leaning against it from the outside.

"Is the girl in there?" Suomi asked. Again no one would answer. He supposed that at this stage it made no difference whether she was or not.

His captors knew somehow which room was his—perhaps they had found his name on something there, perhaps Schoenberg for whatever reason was telling them every small detail. When they thrust Suomi into the room he found it in the same state of disruption as the others he had seen, which was no more than might have been expected after several thorough searches. There was no sign that anything had been wantonly smashed. So much the better.

They left him alone and closed the door behind him; no doubt there would be a soldier leaning against it on the outside. Since the room had not been designed as a prison cell, its door could be locked only from the inside. Unfortunately it had not been designed as a fortress either; though the door was thick and soundproof, it could probably be forced open quickly by a couple of armed and determined men. Nevertheless Suomi quietly activated the lock.

He went then to stand beside his bunk, where an intercom control was set into the wall, and paused with his hand upraised. He could try to reach Barbara this way. But what could he say? Some of the enemy might well be in her room listening. To try to reassure her, to offer hope, might be much worse than useless. He turned the intercom to a position where it would receive but not transmit and left it there.

The next thing he did was to get himself a long drink of cold water from the little sink. Then he opened the medicine chest, selected an antibiotic and a painkiller. There also he found a medicated dressing to put on the worst of his minor wounds, the leg gash that somehow had become infected. After that, with a single glance of longing at the comfortable bunk, he walked to the little desk-workbench where he had kept his personal cameras and sound-recording gear. This material, like everything else, had been looked at and scattered. He opened drawers, looked in corners, searching. All was in disarray, but it seemed that nothing he needed had been removed or broken. He uttered a sigh of relief that broke off midway as he entered a new phase of tension.

It was time to sit down and get to work.

* * *

In its buried shrine far below the Temple the berserker perceived the chanting far above of five familiar male voices. From the same location came the sounds of the shuffling of fourteen human feet, in a pattern consistent with that of one of the processions with which the humans habitually began their sacrificial rituals. Routine analysis of the sounds allowed the berserker to identify among the members of the procession not only five of its familiar servitors but two other human organisms, one male and one female, that were strangers to it.

Compulsively but still routinely, the berserker concentrated all its senses upon the unknown male, who was not stumbling slightly on bare feet at the top of the long stone stair that must be unfamiliar to him, as the procession began its descent from Thorun's temple. As it would have done with any strange male, the berserker was attempting an identification with another whose personal patterns were carried under highest priority in its data banks.

Since its crippling and near-destruction in the battle of 502.78 . . . standard years ago the berserker's senses had been blurred and uncertain, hardly better than human sight and hearing. But the procession was bringing the unknown male nearer and nearer now, and the probability of his being identified with the prime target patterns was rapidly declining to a negligible level. The berserker was free to turn its attention to other matters.

In the electronuclear mind of the berserker

there was no wonder and no impatience, but there was definitely an awareness that some events were far more probable than others. In that sense therefore the berserker was surprised when it computed that today two human victims were to be offered to it instead of one, or an animal only, as often happened.

In all the time since the battle in which it was damaged, since the human goodlife on this planet had rescued it from destruction and begun to offer it worship, the berserker had received such multiple offerings on only a few occasions. Searching back now through its memory banks and comparing data, it noted that these had invariably been times of intense emotion among its devotees.

One such occasion had been the celebration of final victory over a particularly stubborn enemy tribe, a victory attained by following a battle plan computed by the berserker for its worshippers and handed down by it as a divine command. Then seventy-four human organisms, all members of the defeated tribe, had been sacrificed to it in one day. At another time of multiple sacrifice the emotions of those offering it had been much different. Then they were pleading for help, during a period of great food shortage. From that famine the berserker had led its followers and their tribe into a land ripe for plunder, by outlining for them a migration route, using its old battle-maps of the planet's surface. And now it computed that the successful capture of the starship, and the impending completion of the long effort to find a way to sterilize

the planet, must also produce intense emotion
among this generation of its goodlife servants.

The berserker did not understand emotion,
and only when compelled by circumstances
would it try to work with what it did not understand. The stimulus-response patterns called
fear and lust, for example, seemed at first to be
readily computable in humans as well as in less
dangerously intelligent animals. But in more
than five hundred years of attempting to master
human psychology well enough to use these patterns to manipulate human organisms, the
berserker had time and again run into depths
and complexities of behavior that it could not
understand. To accept worship meant trying to
use patterns that were, if anything, even deeper
and more complex, a tremendously uncertain
means of working toward its goal. But no better
means had been available, and with the capture
of the starship it seemed that this was after all
going to prove successful.

Now the procession had completed its descent
of the stair, and now it was entering the
berserker's chamber. The High Priest Andreas
entered first, his vestments for this occasion of
red and black, Thorun's white and purple having been put secretly aside above, in Thorun's
temple. The robes in which the High Priest now
appeared to worship his true god were heavily
and ineradicably stained with the rust-brown of
old blood.

Behind Andreas came Gus De La Torre and
Celeste Servetus, their wrists bound behind

them, garbed in white and garlanded with live
flowers that would soon be scattered on the floor
to die. Four priests of the Inner Circle followed,
their robes for this special occasion red and
black like the High Priest's, and stained like his
as well.

Andreas and the other four men conducting
the sacrifice began performing the usual prostra-
tions and chanting the usual litanies, while the
victims, as usual, watched in uncertainty and
mounting fear. The berserker had long ago
noted that the words and actions used in these
rituals tended to change but little over the standard centuries, the long Hunterian years, only
gradually becoming somewhat more elaborate.
For the moment it kept quiet. It had realized
long ago that the less it said during a sacrificial
ceremony, the better. Not only did it thus lessen
the risk of confusing and disillusioning its worshippers by saying something out of tune with
their incomprehensible psychology, but the rarer
its pronouncements were, the more importance
humans were wont to grant them.

Two of the priests had now picked up instruments of music, and the rhythm of a drum and
the wail of a horn now blended with the chanting. The music ordered and modified the beat of
alpha brain waves, and the rhythms of other
biological processes, in all the humans present.

"Gus, help me! Help! Oh, God, no no nooo!"
So screamed the female upon at last fully per-
ceiving the stained altar just before her, and
evidently realizing its purpose, just at the moment when the two priests who were not playing

instruments came to tear away her garlands and clothes and chain her down upon the stones. The berserker watched steadily to see whether Gus or God (whatever entities these might be) might come to the female's aid, although from its experience following 17,261 similar appeals the probability seemed vanishingly small.

The female was secured to the altar and no help for her arrived. Her screams continued as Andreas took up a sharp implement and removed from her living body the organs most closely connected with the reproduction of life and the nourishment of the very young. These he threw before the berserker, demonstrating a symbolic and real triumph of Death over the very wellsprings of life. The ventral surface of her torso was then opened more deeply, and the central blood-pump of her body was excised, whereupon the female almost instantly ceased to function.

It was now time for the second victim to be placed upon the altar.

"No. Listen, my friends, I'm with you. No, no, not me. How can this be happening? Wait, let's talk, you're making a mistake. I'll join you." And then a wordless, hopeless cry, as his feet were tripped out from under him and he was thrown down naked upon the stones.

Why should the male organism continue to struggle so violently when it must perceive that the chances of such struggle producing favorable results were now astronomically remote? Now at last the male had been chained down.

"I'll help you! I'll do anything you want. Oh.

Ah. No. Forgive me, everyone . . ." Another scream, as his organs of generation too were removed, and cast into the bloody puddle of female parts. And now his ventral tissues parted under the sharp knife in the High Priest's hands, and now his heart, still pulsating, was held up in offering to the god of Death.

"It is well, it is pleasing," the berserker told the five gory, happy men who now stood quietly before it. Drum and horn and voice had ceased. The chamber was still. The five who still bore the burden of life were subsiding now into states of emotional relaxation.

"I am pleased," the berserker reiterated. "Go now and prepare to bring the starship to me, that we may begin to attach my circuitry to its control systems. Only when that is done can we begin the alteration of its drive."

"Today or tomorrow, oh Death, we will bring you the starship," said Andreas. "As soon as we are sure that Lachaise can fly it safely we will lower it into the pit. Tomorrow also we will bring you fresh human sacrifice."

"That will be good." Meanwhile a possible problem had suggested itself to the berserker. "Are many of your people mystified by or curious about the ship? Is there any unrest because of its presence?"

"There is some curiosity about it, oh Death, but I will handle that. This afternoon there will be a distraction that will leave the people able to think or talk of nothing else. Thorun is going to walk forth into the city and display his powers."

The berserker tried to compute the probable

results of such an event, and found it could not grapple with the numerous abstract factors successfully. "In the past you have always been cautious about putting Thorun on display."

"Lord Death, the masses will not accept as divine any creature that they can see daily in the streets. But Thorun's future will now be short in any case. At the most, a thirtieth-of-an-old-man's-lifetime, and the masses of this world will no longer need a god—or any god save Thou."

The berserker decided to trust its goodlife servant in this manner. So far he had never failed his god. "So be it, loyal Andreas. Proceed in the service of Death as you think best."

Andreas bowed low, and then the humans began their rituals of departure, which included cleaning up the mess they had made.

The berserker computed routinely that two deaths had been achieved today, which was a good, if modest, accomplishment. But, as always the waste of time and energy involved in formal sacrifice had been considerable, and that was not good.

Never had the berserker asked for offerings of pain and terror. Killing, simple killing without end as long as life existed, was all it wanted. It was not enthusiastic about inflicting pain, which was after all a manifestation of life and therefore, after all, evil.

It allowed the torture to go on only because the infliction of pain was so satisfying to the humans who were its servitors.

XII

The two finalists of Thorun's Tournament were still being kept waiting outside the city gate.

"Thomas, why are we being treated so? Disregarded. Forced to wait here, like tradesmen or musicians or actors, without honor. Are we not now nearly gods? Is this just some final form of trial?"

"My foolish, highborn friend." Thomas's voice was sympathetic, the rest of his answer long in coming. "You really think that there are gods in there?"

"I—" Farley had not been able to sit down for restlessness, and now he swayed on his feet in agony of mind. "Thorun help me! I do not know." His admission of doubt hung in the air while time stretched on and on, an endless-seeming time for Farley in which, as far as he could tell, Thorun did nothing at all.

"You in there!" Farley bellowed suddenly, toward the priests who still looked down upon them from the wall. Startled eyes swung round

to focus on him. The priest Yelgir had gone in
some time ago, saying he would soon be back.

"What?" one answered, awkwardly.

"Are we companions of the gods or not? What
kind of welcome is this you have prepared for us?
Leros shall hear of this, and the High Priest himself!"

He paused then, as suddenly as if he had run
into a wall, his flaring anger burned out as fast
as it had arisen. "Thomas," he whispered. "Did
you hear my words just now? Not 'Thorun will
hear of this' but 'the High Priest will hear'. I
know now what I believe." Again his look
changed to anger once more, but this time quiet
and bitter. "Why then am I here?"

His loud outburst had had enough effect on
the priests that one of them was now beginning
a speech placatory if not apologetic. But Farley
would not hear it. Still speaking to Thomas, he
demanded: "Tell me, what will happen if you
and I choose not to fight? If we simply turn our
backs on them, and go about our own affairs?"

Thomas was aghast and scowling, shaking his
head in silent disapproval. Farley could bear no
more. With deliberate scorn he turned his back
on all of them and started to walk away. Thomas
at once glanced toward the priests and saw their
wishes in their eyes. Farley had not gone more
than ten paces before Thomas came to block his
way. Not for the first time, it struck Farley as
marvelous that such a bulky man could move so
lightly.

"Thomas, walk away with me, in peace."

The man holding the spear leveled shook his
head. "That cannot be."

"Come. If you still lust for more fighting, I have no doubt that we will find it on our way. These soft men who play at being gods will send their soldiers after us and we are not likely to reach the bottom of the mountain alive. But we will die in true battle, as men should, and not for the amusement of liars. Come."

Thomas was still not angry, but very grim. "Farley, I mean to remain alive, and to prove to these men that I am the mightiest warrior in the land. If I do not conquer you, that will not be proven fully. Come. Let us fight."

The spear had been leveled for some time, and now Farley saw the little movement at Thomas's shoulder that meant a thrust was coming. Farley drew his own weapon even as he leaped back from the spear thrust. Farley fought. There was no choice. When he struck with his sword his arm felt as strong as ever, but something was lacking now—from his backbone or from his soul.

He was not conscious of being afraid. It was only that he wanted nothing but to leave this place of fraud. His feet tried to move him toward the downhill road when they should have been driving him forward for the kill. And suddenly his belly was being torn open by the spear.

Farley knew that he was lying on his face in the soft groundcover. Not bad, his father said, reaching down a hand to help him up, but you must practice more. Oh father, I tried so hard. Then it seemed to Farley that he was walking carefree through the gods' green park, but the white walls were behind him, not in front, and he was going home.

Thomas, when he had made sure that the last loser of the Tournament was quite dead, bent over to once more wipe his spear. He cleaned it on Farley's costly cloak; the cloth had been ruined anyhow, by the days and nights in the open, and the many battles.

When the weapon was as clean as he could get it under the circumstances Thomas attached the carrying cord to the spear again and slung it over his shoulder. The same few faces were still watching him from the gate and the top of the wall. They showed mild approval, like idlers looking on at some casual brawl. None of them said anything.

"Well," Thomas announced, feeling somewhat irritated, "you have seen it. I am your man. Six duels against the very best in the world, and I have only one trifling scratch while they are all dead."

"Andreas will be displeased at missing the final duel," said one. Another called down to Thomas: "Be patient for a little while. The High Priest is coming soon, we expect. Come inside the gate if you wish."

Thomas decided to bring Farley into the city with him, as a trophy, a symbol of all his victories. He squatted and with a grunt picked up the warm, loose body at his feet. Farley was heavier than the appearance of his rangy frame suggested, and Thomas's steps toward the city gate were slow and weighty. The gate swung open for him after he had stood before it for a moment in fast-mounting impatience.

His first view of the city inside was a disappointment. The gate gave directly onto a small paved square, only about twenty meters on a side. The square was completely boxed in by buildings and walls that were but little lower than the outer city wall through which he had just passed. There were several gates in the inner walls, but all were closed, or showed nothing but more walls beyond, so there was not much of interest to be seen in any direction. A few more people, of high and low degree, were looking down at Thomas from walls and windows. Seeing no place in particular to go, Thomas bent and with some care set his slow-dripping burden down.

A small fountain gurgled nearby and he went to get a drink of water, seeing that no one was rushing to offer him fermented milk or wine. The people on the walls had ceased to stare at him now, and were gone about their business. Others appeared from time to time to glance and turn away. Here and there slaves went about their errands. A train of pack animals entered the city through the outer gate which had remained open, and came brushing past Thomas at close quarters.

The man on the wall who had invited him in had gone. Thomas looked about, but there was no one for him to berate for his shabby treatment. Was he expected to go prowling the city at random, grabbing strangers by the arm and asking directions? Where is Thorun's great hall? He is expecting me.

They had said the High Priest was coming. Seating himself on the edge of the fountain,

Thomas retired into dignity, and remained there quietly as the shadows shifted across the square with the slow progress of the sun. Once there intruded upon his thoughts a soft snuffling, lapping sound. A small hungry domestic animal had discovered Farley's otherwise forgotten corpse. Thomas moved fast, took two strides and launched the beast halfway across the square with a rib-cracking kick. Then he returned to the fountain and sat passively waiting.

When at last he heard someone approaching him and looked up ready to speak his anger, he found that it was only Leros, with whom he had no quarrel. Leros looked sick, or at least noticeably older than he had a few days ago.

Standing before him with hands outspread, Leros said: "I am sorry, Thomas, Lord Thomas. They say Andreas is coming now, but I do not know what welcome he plans to give you. If I were High Priest things would be different. Let me congratulate you on your victory."

Thomas got up to his full height. "Where is the High Priest Andreas?" he called out, looking around at the anonymous faces on walls and in windows. Suddenly their number was growing again, more people peering out into the square at every moment. Something impended. Spectators were gathering. "Where is he, I am growing impatient with this treatment."

"Speak more respectfully," a tall, regal-looking man admonished him sharply from his place of security on a high inner wall.

Thomas looked this one over and decided to continue to be bold; it was an attitude that usually got results, for him. "Respectfully? I am a god now, am I not? Or a demigod at least. And you do not look like anything more than a man."

"The point is well taken," said Leros sternly to the man on the wall. That one looked angry, but before he could say anything a murmur swept around the square and everyone's attention again shifted. The smallest and most intricately decorated of the inner gates that gave on the square was being opened from the far side by a young priest. Footsteps crunched on the neat gravel walk revealed beyond this gate, and there emerged from it a tall, skull-faced man dressed more in purple than in white. From the reactions of those around him, Thomas realized that this must be Andreas.

"You must be Thomas the Grabber," the High Priest said, nodding to him affably, speaking in the confident voice of one who is habitually in charge of things. "I see you have finished the Tournament somewhat ahead of schedule. I am sorry to have missed it all—the final round especially. But no matter, Thorun is pleased." Andreas nodded, smiling his smile. "So pleased is he that he has decided to grant you special honor, even beyond that promised you below."

This was more like it. Thomas made a little bow toward the High Priest, then stood taller than before.

The smile was a baring of teeth in the skull mouth. "You are to fight the fight that all true warriors must dream about. I hope that you are ready. But of course, as a true warrior, you must be."

"I am ready," Thomas growled, meanwhile
cursing himself mentally for being fooled by the
first soft words. "But I am done with fighting, as
far as Thorun's Tournament is concerned. I am
the winner." All around him he heard a catching
of breaths. Evidently one did not talk like that to
the master of the world, the High Priest of
Thorun. But Thomas would not simply bow his
head and be only another man, not now. He
must take and hold the place that he rightfully
earned.

Andreas, glaring at him, put steel into his
voice. "You are to fight against Thorun himself.
Do you mean that you would prefer to enter his
hall with your blood still safe inside your veins,
with all your joints still hung together? I cannot
believe it."

The murmuring voices rose up wildly now, in
rumor and speculation. What did the High
Priest mean? Could Thorun actually be coming,
to duel against a mortal man?

It made no sense to Thomas, and he did not
like it in the least. Still, looking at the clever and
experienced Andreas, very much in control, he
decided that boldness had its limits. He bowed
once more to the High Priest, and said: "Sir, a
word with you alone, if I may."

"No more words, for you or from you," said
Andreas softly. He turned his head slightly in a
listening gesture, and smiled again.

Beyond the gateway through which Andreas
had come the gravel crunched again, in the
rhythm of a single long-striding pair of feet. Incredibly heavy the tread must be, to make the

gravel sound like that. Above the low wall in that
direction the top of a head came into view, a mat
of wild dark hair, while the feet must be moving
at ground level three meters lower. No man was
that tall. With an unfamiliar weakness in his
knees Thomas believed for a moment that his
own cynicism had undone him after all. The
naive pious ones had been right all along. The
dead of the Tournament, dismembered and
buried and burnt along the way, would shortly
walk before him, laughing as they followed—

The figure now appearing in the gateway
before Thomas, bending to pass through.

Thorun.

XIII

His head of wild dark hair was bound up by a golden band. His fur cloak, vast as it was, barely covered his mountainous shoulders. His marvelous sword, nearly as long as Thomas's spear, was girdled to his waist. All as the legends had it. His face, though . . .

Thorun did not seem to be looking at anything. He stared over Andreas's head, and over Thomas's, and through the still-open outer gate (where the limping maul-slave stood and gaped as if he thought those eyes were fixed on him) and brooded with his terrible unblinking eyes upon the world outside. Once he had come to a halt Thorun did not move, did not shift his position or stir a finger, any more than would a statue.

Andreas said nothing more, or, if he did so, Thomas did not hear. Rather the High Priest bowed himself out of the way, silently and obsequiously, though with some amusement still visible, out of the way of the mighty figure of the god.

The eyes had moved now, though the head

had not, and Thorun was looking at Thomas. The eyes had literally some kind of glow inside them, like those of an animal seen at nighttime by reflected light. This glow was red and orange. Glancing quickly around, Thomas saw that the eyes were on him alone, for no one any longer stood near him. Against one wall of the square he saw Leros prostrate in deep reverence, as were a number of others on walls and ground.

Scores of men were watching now, men in white robes and gray rags. Those who had been in the middle of the square were scrambling away, reaching for high perches, getting out of the way. Awe was in every face. Almost. Only Farley would not interrupt his contemplation of the sky.

Thorun now came stepping forward. Though his movements were limber and seemed natural enough, even graceful, for some reason the impression of watching a statue persisted. Perhaps it was the face, which was utterly inhuman, though the form of each individual feature was correct. Neither was the face godlike—unless gods were less than men, unless they were not, in fact, alive.

But Thorun's strides were very long and purposeful. Thomas, seeing the long sword coming endlessly out of its scabbard as the god approached, got himself into motion just in time. The man launched himself backward out of the arc of the sword, and it made a soft and mournful sighing as it passed in a stroke that would have cut a man in half as readily as a weed. The war god's bearded lips opened at last and bellowed forth a deafening battle-cry. It was a strange and terrible sound, as inhuman as the glowing, unblinking eyes and the dead face.

Getting his spear unlimbered just in time, Thomas mechanically held it out to parry Thorun's next stroke. When the god's sword struck he felt a numbing jolt up both his arms, and his armored spear was nearly torn out of his grasp. It was like some nightmare of being a child again, and facing a grown warrior in combat. The watchers cheered. Whoever or whatever Thorun was, his strength was well beyond that of any man.

Thorun advanced methodically, unhurriedly. Backing and circling, Thomas knew that he must now plan and fight the finest battle of his life.

Thomas began to fight his finest battle but before long was forced to realize that it was hopeless. His own most violent attacks were knocked aside with effortless ease, while Thorun's sword strokes came with such murderous power and precision that he knew he could not parry or avoid them for long. Already the battering of sword on spear had made his arms grow numb and weary. He was gripping his spear in both hands like a quarterstaff and retreating steadily, meanwhile trying to discover some workable strategy, to spy out some weakness in the defense of his monstrous opponent. Whether that opponent was god or man or something else entirely was a question that did not bother Thomas in the least just now.

At last, with a good deceptive move followed by a superb thrust, Thomas got his spear-point home into Thorun's tunic of heavy fur, only to feel it rebound from some hard layer of armor underneath. A moment of sudden hope burned out as quickly as it had come. Around him the watchers gasped in astonishment at his seeming success, then relaxed with a collective sigh as the world, that had tilted for a moment, settled back. Thorun was unconquerable.

Thomas, however, retained a spark of hope. If he could hit home once with the spear, then he might be able to hit home again. If the fur-clad chest and belly were invulnerable, where should he try to strike?

How about the face? No. He could stand a little farther off—and it would be less nearly suicidal—if he tried instead for the legs. Thomas observed that the joints of Thorun's exposed and seemingly unarmored knees were not covered with unbroken skin like that on human legs, but instead showed fine and smoothly shifting cracks, as if they were the legs of a well-made puppet. The opening in the knee-joint presented a very small and moving target, but no more difficult a one than the insects on the wing Thomas had sometimes hit in practice.

No better plan having suggested itself, Thomas feinted high, low, high again, and then put all his power and skill into a low thrust. His eyes and arms did not fail him. The sharp point of the spear found the small opening just as it was narrowing slightly with the straightening of Thorun's leg.

There came a grinding vibration down the spear's shaft, and an audible snap of metal. Thorun lurched but did not fall. With the slamming of a door, a silence fell over the arena. The tip of Thomas's spearhead came away bright, where its point had been broken off.

The silence that had fallen when Thorun nearly lost his footing still held; Thorun's knee was now frozen in a half-bent position. The ruler of the world was wounded, and nothing could be heard but the scraping dragging of his crippled foot as he continued to advance. He advanced more slowly than before but as implacably as ever. Thomas, in retreat again, glimpsed Andreas standing atop a wall. The High Priest's face was dark as a thundercloud, and one of his hands was half extended like a claw, as if he wanted to interfere now but did not dare.

The limping god came in range again of his human opponent. Once more Thorun's great sword became a gleaming blur of speed, hammering on with untiring violence, driving Thomas back and back, around and around the little space. Thomas, meaning to strike again at the wounded knee, feinted high and low and high again, and then was nearly killed, was knocked off his feet, by the impact of the sword against his spear. Thorun was not to be fooled twice by the same tactic.

Thomas rolled over desperately. Thorun, lurching with grotesque speed, was almost upon him. Thomas got his feet under him and got away barely in time. Leap in and grab, Thomas? Never, against this foe. As well leap in and wrestle an ice-born glacier-beast—or one of the glaciers themselves.

Somehow Thomas had managed to retain his spear, and he was still blocking the sword with its steel-armored shaft, but he could no longer gather energy to launch a thrust. Still the sword drove him back and back, and around and around. Now the watching white-robes had once more found their voices.

The end could not be held off any longer, Thomas thought. Weary and off balance, he raised his arms in desperation to catch yet another swordsweep against his indestructible spear. Again the impact knocked him from his feet. The world seemed to turn slowly, slowly around him as he spun in the air and fell, giving him time to wonder whether there was a real Thorun to be confronted after he had been slain by this limping imposter.

Thomas came down hard and for a moment could not move. He had lost his grip on his spear at last. The weapon lay only a handsbreadth from his fingers in the dust of the square, but grasping it again was one of the hardest greatest achievements of Thomas's life.

The killing machine paused in its limping progress, as if uncertain whether the fight was already won. Then with its crablike motion it came forward once again. Thomas got himself up on one knee, his spear leveled. Another sudden cessation of noise made him aware of how the watchers had been yelling for his death. Thorun's glowing but lifeless eyes were judging

him. What was the wargod waiting for? Thomas
struggled back to his feet, knowing that the next
swordstroke, or the one after that, would surely
be the last. Then with the edge of his vision he
saw a gray-clad figure approaching him from
one side. It moved with a limp, as if in sacri-
ligious mockery of wounded Thorun's gait. The
slave's leaden maul was lifting casually to dash
out Thomas's brains.

Thomas had been ready to meet death, but by
all the gods, this was too much! He was not yet
down and helpless! He turned, meaning to spear
the slave through, while Thorun, lackwit, continued to hesitate.

Muscles ready for a killing lunge, Thomas for
the first time looked closely into the slave's face,
and was momentarily paralyzed by what he saw.
And gray-clad Giles the Treacherous stepped
sideways with smooth unlimping speed, and
with all his warrior's strength let fly with the
massive maul against Thorun's already damaged knee.

Metal cracked. The bright arc of Thorun's
next swordstroke, already underway, went tilting awkwardly and curved well wide of Giles and
Thomas both. Metallic snapping sounds prolonged themselves. Slowly, but without dignity,
the monster sat down, its left knee bent at a
wrong angle. It came to rest in a sitting position
with its torso bolt upright, staring at its enemies
with a face that had not changed, but had suddenly become absurd.

"Thomas!" cried Giles. He leaped back just
in time from the next stroke that Thorun, still

sitting, aimed at him. "Get him between us, Thomas. Finish him!"

For the first time uttering a war-cry of his own, a hoarse and wordless yell, Thomas moved quickly to accomplish the encirclement. His peripheral vision told him that no one in the watching throng was moving to interfere. They were in pandemonium, their white robes swirling with disordered motion and their voices straining in excited noise. There was Leros, standing with arms folded in apparent calm, barely out of the way of the fight and watching it in utter concentration. Thomas glimpsed Andreas standing on a wall. The High Priest was waving his arms and seemed to be shouting orders, but the insane excitement was now such that no man's voice could be heard.

Even crippled as he was Thorun came near to being a match for his opposition. Neither spear nor maul could beat down the huge sword in his untiring arm, and he turned his seated body with marvelous speed to face first one foreman and then the other.

Catching the eye of Giles, Thomas roared: "Together! Now!" and they rushed at Thorun from opposite sides simultaneously. The sword came at Thomas, and he managed to parry it yet again only because Thorun, in his sitting position, could not get his whole body behind a swing. Even so Thomas thought for a moment that his own forearm had been broken in the clash. But meanwhile Giles had got in close, swinging like a piledriver, and landed his maul full force on the back of Thorun's neck.

The blow would have exploded the head of

any mortal man. Thorun's wild hair flew, his
great head jerked, his torso swayed a little,.his
swordarm hesitated. Now Thomas's blunted
spearpoint smashed into his right eye, which
went out like a candle, with a tiny crunch that
came through the spear like breaking glass. Now
the maul came down again, this time on the
swordhand. Thorun did not drop his sword, but
now it stood out at a different angle from his fist.

The giant died slowly, piecemeal, indifferent
rather than brave, emitting neither cries not
blood. There was only a step-by-step loss of
function under the terrible punishment of spear
and hammer, a progressive revelation of
Thorun's vincibility, a bit-by-bit reduction of his
body to little more than shattered metal and
glass and fur.

Even when the huge body was hopelessly
beaten, when the god's battered face had been
humiliatingly pounded down into the earth
beside the fountain, the sword arm was still
trying to fight, lashing out with murderous, random blows. A spear thrust loosened its fingers
and the giant sword fell from the hand with a
dull little sound. The arm, its broken digits
clutching spasmodically on emptiness, was still
waving when Thomas and Giles looked at each
other, rested their weapons, and then turned together to salute the watchers who ringed them
in.

The noise of the crowd died away into an exhausted silence, a silence that seemed to Thomas
to go on for a very long time. Andreas was no
longer to be seen, he noted, and a few others had
also vanished. Most were still watching, as if

hypnotized, the helpless, stubborn movements of
Thorun's arm. Thomas went to kick the huge
sword out of its reach.

Eyes began now to turn toward Leros, who was
the senior priest still in attendance. Obviously in
the grip of powerful emotions, he took two steps
forward and stretched forth an arm toward the
fallen giant; but Leros was still too overcome to
speak, and the fist of his outstretched arm
clenched tightly, his arm dropped back to his
side.

It was left to Giles to break the silence at last.
Gesturing at the wrecked giant, he shouted out:
"This creature is not your beloved Thorun. It
cannot be! Andreas and his Inner Circle have
deceived you all!"

The roar that went up from the crowd in response had much of agreement in it. But one
voice cried out to Giles: "Who are you, that have
interfered and done this? Agent of the Brotherhood! Spy!"

Giles raised a hand and got silence in which to
make his answer. "Very well, say I am a spy, an
agent, anything you like. But what I have shown
you here is nothing but the truth. Call me what
you will. But will you call me a god, to defeat
another god in combat? And what god could I
be, to conquer Thorun?" He raised his face to
the bright sky, and made a holy sign. "Great
Thorun, avenge yourself upon the blasphemers
who have put forth this deception!" And he
gestured again to where ruined Thorun still
moved one arm in a parody of battle.

Several men with their daggers drawn—there

were no larger weapons in evidence among the crowd—came to surround Giles. They took away his maul and stood guard over him, but at a word from Leros did no more. Giles made no protest or resistance, but stood proudly with his arms folded. Leros, after gazing a little while longer in continued shock at what remained of Thorun, summoned two or three other leaders who were present to withdraw with him to a corner of the square. There they at once plunged into earnest talk. Most of the other spectators, marveling and arguing, began to crowd around the fallen figure that had been their god.

Giles the Treacherous, looking at Thomas, suddenly flashed him a smile of surprising brightness for a man in his doubtful situation. "Lord Thomas," Giles hailed him, "it seems that you are now the champion of gods as well as men."

"Well. You don't claim a share of the prize, whatever it may prove to be?" Thomas moved closer to Giles, with whom he felt a kinship.

"I? Never. You have won the championship fairly and I have no claim to make."

Thomas nodded, satisfied on this point. But he had other worries. Standing next to Giles, he looked around him restlessly. He had the feeling that as champion of the Tournament, and acknowledged victor over the imitation Thorun, he should be doing something, asserting authority somehow. Probably he should go to join the talk around Leros and make the priests listen to him. But what would he tell them? He realized now that he had not the faintest idea of what was really going on. He was more likely to find out, he thought, if he stayed with Giles, who might well need some help in return soon and be willing to bargain. Anyway, Thomas felt much more at home talking with another fighting man than he did with the priests.

"Why are you here, and how?" he asked the shorter man. "It is in my memory that I saw you die."

Giles's smile had faded to a mere twist of the lip. "You saw Jud thrust at me, and me go plunging down a hillside."

"You were not even wounded?"

"I was not. You see, I had persuaded Jud that all I wanted was a chance to get out of the Tournament and away. He was something of a cynic, and so believed me. Also he was glad of the chance to take an uncontested victory, and went along with the plan I had hatched. He had only to hold back his thrusts a little, as I did.

"His sword only took a few threads from my jacket before I went over the edge. I had marked beforehand that the slave carrying the maul was of my size and coloring, which suggested the whole plan to me. When the slave came down to make sure I was dead I was waiting in the bushes and did the office for him instead. I took his rags and his rope belt and his maul, and put them on together with his limp, before dragging him uphill to be buried in my good clothes. The rest of you had started on ahead by then, as I had expected.

"I was seldom in your camp after that. My companion slave was dumb, and so lackwit he did not notice the transformation—or perhaps he was shrewd enough to ignore intrigue when he became aware of it. None of the rest of you ever looked at me with open eyes, once I had put on gray rags—not until you looked at me just now, when you thought I was coming for you with the maul."

Thomas shook his head in wonderment. "A fearful risk you took."

"Not so great a risk as having to face you, or Kelsumba perhaps, or Farley, in open combat. I had made up my mind that *that* risk was too high."

"But still, a strange game," Thomas commented. "Why did you play it? Why—?" He gestured toward the wreckage that had been Thorun.

"I wanted to expose that thing for what it was. Rather, for what it is, since we have so far destroyed only a small part of it." Giles looked around him. His audience, that had been only Thomas and a couple of dagger-guards when he started speaking, was now far larger. He raised his voice and went on: "We all know now that this thing was never Thorun. It was only a creation of something else. Something else whose harboring on Hunters' planet would bring scorn and derision from the whole outworld if it were known to them."

"What is this shameful thing you speak of?" The question came from Leros, who had ended his conference with the other ranking priests and had now been listening to Giles for some little time.

"I am speaking of one of our ancestors' ancient enemies, a berserker," said Giles, and briefly outlined his conversation with Suomi in the woods. "If Andreas has not yet silenced the outworlders he is holding in the Temple, they will be able to confirm that he has stolen their ship from them. Perhaps they will be able to tell us why."

"Why should he believe the outworlders over the High Priest?" someone called, challenging.

Giles raised his voice again. "The outworlders did not bring this imitation Thorun with them. Andreas and his Inner Circle priests have used it for years, to dupe Thorun's faithful followers. No artisan on Hunters' could have made it alone, any more than he could build a spaceship. Nor can it be the true persona of a god, or not even Thomas the Grabber could have knocked it down. What else can it be then, but a berserker, or part of one? If it is not a berserker, perhaps the High Priest and his Inner Circle can explain just what it is. I would ask them now if they were here. But they fled when the saw that their fancy machine was doomed."

Leros nodded grimly. "It is time, and past time, for us to ask Andreas some hard questions." The roar of agreement that went up was short, for men wanted to hear what Leros was going to say next. He went on: "I think, though, that it is not for you to tell us what to ask. Whose agent are you, treacherous one?"

Giles shrugged, and admitted readily: "I was sent here by what you call the Brotherhood. But what of that, honest Leros? Today I have told you and shown you nothing but demonstrable truth. I see now that we of the Brotherhood real- ly have no quarrel with the people of Godsmountain, but only with the Inner Circle and its head."

Leros grunted, perhaps a bit bewildered by the ready flow of words, half convinced by them and half put off by their smoothness. Before he had to reply, however, he was distracted by the return of a man who had evidently been dispatched to see what was going on at the Temple. This messenger brought back word that the doors and gates leading to the Temple complex had been locked and barred from within, and the palace guard of soldiers directly under the command of the High Priest were occupying the place. Andreas would not appear, but only sent out word that all spies, traitors, and their dupes would soon tremble before his wrath.

"He will not answer reasonable questions?" Leros demanded. "He will not explain why he dared to foist this . . . this *thing* . . . upon us as a god?"

"No, Lord Leros, he will not."

"Then it is certain," Leros shouted, "Andreas no longer speaks in Thorun's name! Great Thorun, stand with us now! Stand with us as we prepare to prove in combat who can serve you best!"

There was a new outbreak of shouts and prayers, a general uproar of activity as men rushed to arm themselves, debated hasty plans of organization, and argued over whether any of the military commanders known to be nearly in the field should be summoned with their troops and asked or ordered to drive Andreas from the Temple. Their last suggestion was shouted down. Thomas gathered that the soldiers now in

the Temple were too small a force to hold it for
long against the aroused citizenry. Well, let the
strategists debate; he would know what to do
when it came to fighting.

Finding himself for the moment more or less
alone again with Giles, Thomas said to him: "I
thank you for stepping in against the monster; I
will not forget it." Thomas was beginning to appreciate how shrewd Giles was, and to understand that he himself was going to need shrewd
advice to secure a position of power among these
people.

"You are welcome, Lord Thomas, for whatever my help was worth."

"Why did the Brotherhood send you here?"

Giles made a little self-deprecating motion
with his head. "I was the best fighter they could
find. I was sent to the Tournament from a district largely under their control. They hoped of
course that I could win the Tournament, and
then function against Godsmountain from some
place of authority inside it. But long before the
Tournament was over I realized that I was not
going to win. You and some of the other fighters
were obviously better than I. So I hatched the
scheme using Jud Isaksson . . . but tell me, Lord
Thomas, why are you here?"

"I?" Thomas was surprised.

"Yes. I don't think you ever believed there was
a real Thorun here, to reward you with immortality. I have told you my real reason for taking part in the Tournament; what was yours?"

"Huh. Well, fighting is my business. It was
dangerous, yes, as any real fighting is, but I expected to win. I have never met the man who

could stand against me in single combat."

Giles was quietly fascinated. "Did you never stop to think that each of us could truthfully have made that identical claim? Each of the original sixty-four?"

Thomas blinked. "No," he said slowly. "No, I did not stop to think of that." Suddenly he remembered the utter astonishment on the beardless dying face of young Bram. Was that in the second round or the third? He could not remember, but it seemed very long ago.

He raised a hand over his shoulder to caress the heavy spear slung on his back. He would have to get a new one made. Not only was the point of this one broken but the shaft was dented and weakened, its steel reinforcing strips twisted and loosened by the battering of Thorun's sword. "I wanted a place of power, wanted to be one of the men who rule the world from this mountaintop."

Giles prompted: "You thought they held the Tournament because they wanted the best fighter in the world up here, to be Godsmountain's champion. And as such you would have great power and wealth."

"Yes. That's about it."

"An intelligent guess, I would say. I, too, believed the Tournament had some such purpose, though there were some points I could not understand . . . anyway, it seems that we were wrong. Andreas and his Inner Circle deceived everyone in one way or another. The simple warriors with a simple story of gods, and us by letting us think that we were wise and understood the truth."

Thomas swore a great oath, throwing in all the gods he could remember on short notice. "Then why *did* they have the Tournament? Andreas and his gang did not watch us to applaud our skill or dwell upon our sufferings. Nobody was allowed to watch, except for a few priests and the outworlders. Why, why preach and urge us on to slaughter one another?"

"They wanted senseless slaughter," said Giles, "because they really do not worship Thorun, who has life and honor in him, and a purpose besides destruction. They could never get the mass of people to worship their true god, who is nothing but Death. Thorun enjoys women and wine, tall tales and food. Especially he honors the courage that makes all other virtues possible. But death is what *they* worship, and death is what berserkers represent, death without honor or purpose, death alone." Giles fell silent, squinting at the wreckage of Thorun on the ground where it lay face down in the mud near the fountain, not far from Farley's sky-gazing corpse. Then Giles added: "No, that is not good enough. You are right, why did Andreas and the others not watch the Tournament, enjoy the killing—or let others watch it. Only the outworlders were allowed to come . . . and while they watched, their ship was stolen. Is that it? The finest heroes of our planet fought and died only to lure them here."

A shout was being raised by many voices, not only in the square but all around the city. The outworlders' ship was in the air.

XIV

The liftoff when it came was very smooth, and took Suomi completely by surprise; he had dozed off at his desk, his head resting on his arms, and on first waking had had the hideous feeling that the ship was already settling down, its flight completed, and that his only chance to act had come and gone.

Hastily he turned to look at the monitor screen on the bulkhead beside the stateroom's intercom control and saw with relief that the flight was certainly not over. Imaged in the screen now was *Orion*'s control room. The high-ranking priest called Lachaise was seated in the central pilot's chair, bent forward over controls and instruments in an attitude of rigid concentration. Around Lachaise other priests and soldiers sat or stood in nervous postures, clinging to whatever solid supports they could get hold of. Looking past the far side of the control room, Suomi could see down the passageway to the entrance lock, at the far side of which the main exterior hatch was still standing open; moving the ship in such a configuration was perfectly feasible, provided of course that no high speed or high altitude was attained. Another soldier clung just inside the entrance lock, looking out and down through the open outer doors. Presumably he was posted there as insurance should the screens in the control room somehow fail, or (what was much more likely) should the novice pilot have trouble in interpreting their images.

The flight was evidently going to be a short one. The berserker must be somewhere nearby, and its loyal human servants were going to bring the captured starship to it. Then they would be able to get to work in earnest on the ship. Directing an operation on itself, the berserker could be wired into the onboard computers, assimilate them into its brain, and take over the ship's various systems as extensions of its own being. And then the drive . . . its conversion to a death machine could be performed at Godsmountain if convenient, or the berserker could fly itself and a loyal coterie to some safe spot in the uninhabited north and there prepare to kill the world.

Through his stateroom screen Suomi could monitor much of what was showing on the big screens in the control room. He had not dozed long, for it was still bright day outside. He watched, on the screens, the wooded slopes of Godsmountain falling away very gently, then tilting a bit. At the same time Suomi felt *Orion* tilt in the hands of her inexpert pilot as he started her moving sideways toward the summit. They would not be bothering with the artificial gravity on this low, slow flight in atmosphere.

The voices of the people in the control room, and those who were communicating with them from outside the ship, were audible in Suomi's stateroom, coming in over intercom. "Schoenberg," Lachaise was saying tensely now, "I have a yellow light showing on the life-systems panel. Can you explain it?"

"Let me see," said Schoenberg's voice, wearily, speaking offstage from Suomi's viewpoint. After a little pause, presumably while a screen was switched to give him a better view, Schoenberg continued: "That's nothing to worry about. Just a reminder that the main hatch is open and the safety interlocks have been disconnected to let you fly her that way. It's just a reminder so you don't forget and go shooting up into space." Whatever pressure had been brought to bear, Schoenberg was evidently cooperating fairly thoroughly.

The ship was directly over the city now, drifting ballon-like on silent engines only a few meters above the tallest rooftops. "Go higher, Lachaise!" another man's voice barked, authoritatively, and Suomi saw the high-ranking priest in white and purple swivel nervously in the pilot's chair, his pale hands in jerky motion, over-correcting. The ship lurched upward while the men around Lachaise clung to their chairs and stanchions and eyed him apprehensively. The upward acceleration ceased, the ship hung for a heart-stopping moment in free fall, and then with a few more up-and-down oscillations was brought back under more or less steady control.

"I should have been allowed more time to practice!" the pilot protested feverishly.

"There is no time," the authoritative voice snapped back. Suomi recognized it now as that of Andreas, speaking from outside the ship. "Thorun failed and Leros and some agent of the Brotherhood have inflamed the mob. We will load our dear lord and master onto the ship and take him to safety in the north with our prisoners. All will yet be well, Lachaise, if you can only maneuver carefully. Come over the Temple now."

Lachaise was now guiding himself by a screen that showed what was directly below the ship. Suomi, in effect looking over Lachaise's shoulder, saw a strange sight the significance of which he could not grasp at first. Near the largest building in the center of the city—this must be the Temple, for the ship was now hovering almost directly above it—another much lower structure was having its roof peeled back, dismantled, from inside. The workmen doing the job were partly visible, their hands and arms coming and going, removing pieces of roof from the edge of the rapidly enlarging opening. Inside there was the tracery of thin scaffolding on which the workmen evidently stood, and besides that nothing but darkness, unconquerable by the sun that everywhere else fell bright on street and wall. It took Suomi a few moments to realize that the building's interior looked dark because it was a single vast pit, dug far below the level of the city's streets.

"Tell them to hurry with the roof," Lachaise pleaded.

"Are you in position yet?" the voice of Andreas countered, the strain in it now quite audible. "I do not think you are quite in the proper position."

Suomi could see now that small but tumultuous groups of white-robed men were running about in the streets around the Temple complex, deploying as if to encircle it. Here and there a drawn sword waved. And uniformed soldiers moved about on the Temple's walls. Now Suomi saw the bright streak of an arrow flying from street to wall and two more darting in the opposite direction in reply. Perhaps the man in gray, with his grandiose scheme of entering the city disguised as a slave and touching off a rebellion, had been more successful than Suomi had thought possible.

As for Suomi himself, he had done all he could at the workbench and now it was time to prepare for combat. Feeling unreal, he picked up the small battery-powered unit he had assembled and went quickly across the small room and got into his bunk. Reaching up an arm, he turned his intercom to SPEAK. The voices of the others still came in; and, though they still could not see him, he could join in their conversation now. But he was not ready.

The bunk was capable of being converted into an acceleration couch, meant to be used in case of failure of artificial gravity somewhere in deep space. To fully convert the bunk now would not be feasible, but Suomi swung the center section of restraining pads over himself as he lay down, and locked it into place. He lay there holding his

little recorder ready to play, the gain turned to
maximum. He lay rigid with tension and fear,
almost unable to breathe, not yet knowing for
certain whether he would be brave enough to do
what must be done. That it might kill him was
not so bad. That it might accomplish nothing
except to earn him a leisurely and hideous punishment from a victorious Andreas—that was
very possible, and a chance just about too hideous to take.

Suomi, by turning his head, could still observe
his stateroom screen. Lachaise was edging the
ship over the great pit now, unmistakably meaning to lower it inside. The removal of the roof out
to the eaves had been completed. The fragile
scaffolding left inside would part like spiderweb
beneath *Orion*'s armored weight. It was all very
well planned and organized. Andreas and the
others must have been preparing for a long time
to capture a starship. Who had told them how to
plan their pit, how big it must be to hold the
kind of ship men would be likely to use on a sur-
reptitious hunting expedition? Of course, their
lord and beloved master, Death . . . Death knew
all the sizes and shapes of human starships, he
had fought against them for a thousand years.

Lachaise in his pilot's chair was now carrying
on a continuous exchange of tense comments
with the men waiting and guiding him below,
and with the lookout at the open hatch. The ship
began to lower. Down, and down—but this
proved to be a false start, and Lachaise had to
straighten her out and bring her up again, drib-
bling a thin trail of white dust from where the

hard hull had brushed delicately against a high
Temple cornice and knocked down a barrowful
or two of masonry.

Up they went, and sideways an almost im-
perceptible distance, and started down again.
Lachaise was probably a natural technician and
machine operator; at any rate he was learning
very fast. This time the slow descent was true.

His finger on the switch that would turn on
the recorder, Suomi balanced over infinite
depths of personal change, chasms of sudden
death or slow defeat and somewhere a small
plateau of triumph. With a part of his mind he
wondered if this was the sensation that Schoenberg and other hunters sought, and the men who
faced one another in the Tournament, when a
lifetime's awareness of being seemed to pulse
through every second of experience.

He could accept all the possibilities. He could
do what must be done. The ship was going down
into the hole. Timing, now, tactics. At the bottom they might very well cut off the drive, so that
would be too long to wait. Right now, just entering the top of the hole, they were still more outside than in, right now would be too soon.

He waited through an eternity; the ship must
now be a quarter of the way down.

Halfway down. Eternity was passing.

Now. With a relief almost unbearable with
surcease of mental strain, Suomi touched the
switch on the small box he was holding.

The voice of Johann Karlsen, biting and unforgettable, heavily amplified, boomed out

through *Orion*'s intercom system, through the radio links from the control room to the outside, through the open main hatch, reverberating at a volume that must have carried into all the nearby city: "THIS IS THE HIGH COMMANDER SPEAKING. LANDING PARTIES READY. UNCOVER THE BERSERKER . . ."

There was more, but it was drowned out by another voice, a voice that could only be the berserker's own, booming and bellowing from some hidden place: "FULL DRIVE. ANDREAS, IN THE NAME OF GLORIOUS DEATH, FULL DRIVE AT ONCE KILL JOHANN KARLSEN, HE IS PROBABLY ABOARD. I COMMAND YOU, LACHAISE, FULL DRIVE AT ONCE. KILL JOHANN KARLSEN, KIL—"

And then that voice too was buried, drowned out, obliterated by the explosive violence resulting from the full-power application of a starship's drive, not only deep within a planet's gravitational well but almost literally buried within Godsmountain's mass. Suomi, heavily protected by his padded bunk and bracing himself as well as he was able, was still shaken as if by the jaws of a glacier-beast, flattened against the bulkhead next to his bunk, then forced away from it again, only saved by his straps from being smeared against the stateroom's opposite bulkhead. The room's regular lights went out, and simultaneously an emergency light glared into life above the door.

There followed a sudden cessation of acceleration, a silence and a falling that went on and on. Then the fall ended with another bone-jarring crash, loud and violent but still far closer to the humanly endurable on the scale of physical events than was that first detonation drive.

The ship seemed to bounce, crashed again, teetered and rocked, and came at last to a shuddering rest, her decks tilted at somewhere near forty degrees from the horizontal. Now all was quiet. The screen in Suomi's stateroom was effectively dead, its surface only flickering here and there with electronic noise.

Suomi unstrapped himself from his bunk and climbed the crazy slope of the deck to reach the door. He had failed to pick up loose objects before entering combat and breakage in the stateroom had been heavy, though there were no indications of basic structural damage. The strength of the hull had probably saved the ship from that.

The stateroom door opened forcefully when he unlatched it, and the dead or unconscious body of a soldier slid in, trailing broken-looking legs. Suomi stuck his head out into the passage and looked and listened. All was quiet and nothing moved in the glare of the emergency lights. Here too deck and bulkheads and overhead were still in place.

He turned back to the fallen sentry and decided that the man was probably dead. Guilt or triumph might come later, he supposed. Right now Suomi only considered whether to arm himself with the man's sword, which was still resting peacefully in its scabbard. In the end Suomi left it there. A sword in his hand was not going to do any good for anybody, least of all himself.

He thumped on the door of Barbara Hurtado's stateroom and when a weak voice answered he opened the door and climbed in. Amid a kaleidoscopic jumble of multicolored clothes from a spilled closet she sat in a heap on the floor, wearing an incongruous fluffy robe, her brown hair in wild disarray, leaning against a chair that must be fastened to the deck.

"I think my collarbone is broken," she said faintly. "Maybe it isn't, though. I can move my arm."

"I'm the one who did it," he said, "Sorry. There was no way I could give you any warning."

"You?" She raised her eyebrows. "All right. Did you do as much damage to those sons of beasts out there?"

"More, I hope. That was the idea. Shall we go out and see? Can you walk?"

"Love to go and see their broken bodies, but I don't think I can. They've got me chained to my bunk, which I guess is why I wasn't killed. The things they were making me do. Always wondered what soldiers were like and I finally found out."

"I'm going out to look around."

"Don't leave me, Carlos."

Things in the control room were very bad, or very good, depending on your point of view. It was closer to the drive than the staterooms were, Suomi supposed. Lachaise, strapped into the central, padded chair, was leaning back with eyes open and arms outflung, showing no wounds but very plainly dead all the same. Intense localized neutron flux at the moment when the drive's fields collapsed was one possibility in such disasters, Suomi remembered reading somewhere. Lachaise had perished happily, no doubt, in blind obedience to his god, perhaps believing or hoping that he really was killing Johann Karlsen. In the name of glorious death . . . yes.

Around Lachaise, the priests and soldiers who had been helping and watching him had not been strapped into padded chairs. Neutrons or not, they now looked like so many bad losers in the Tournament. This many lives at least had the berserker harvested today. Some of them still breathed, but none were at all dangerous any more.

The main hatch was still open, Suomi discovered, looking down at it from the control room, but it was completely choked with broken white masonry and massive splintered timbers; part of the Temple or of somebody's house perhaps. The ship had come to rest within the city, then. Probably a number of people had been killed outside the ship as well as in it, but Godsmountain had not been leveled, a lot of its people were doubtless still alive, and whoever was left in charge should come digging his way into the ship eventually, probably wanting to take vengeance for the destruction.

With some difficulty Suomi made his way back to Barbara's stateroom and managed to lodge himself in a sitting position by her side. "Exit's blocked. Looks like we wait together."

He described the carnage briefly.

"Be a good boy, Carlos, get me a pain pill from my medicine chest, and a drink."

He jumped up. "Of course. I didn't think— sorry. Water?"

"First. Then one of the other kind, if everything in my bar isn't smashed."

They were still sitting there together, about half a standard hour later, when after much noise of digging and scraping from the direction of the entrance hatch, Leros and a troop of armed men, swords in hand and in full battle gear, appeared in the stateroom's open door. Suomi, who had been listening fatalistically to their approach, looked up at Leros and then closed his eyes, unable to watch the sword's descent.

Nothing descended on him. He heard nothing but a faint multiple clinking and jangling, and opened his eyes to see Leros and his followers facing him on their knees, genuflecting awkwardly on the tilted deck. Among them, looking scarcely less awed than the rest, was the man in gray, armed now with sword instead of hammer.

"Oh Lord Demigod Johann Karlsen," said Leros with deep reverence, "you who are no robot, but a living man, and more, forgive us for not recognizing you when you walked among us! And accept our eternal gratitude for again confounding our ancient enemies. You have smashed the death-machine within its secret lair, and most of those who served it also. Be pleased to know that I myself have cut out the heart of the arch-traitor Andreas."

It was Barbara who—perhaps—saved him then. "The Lord Karlsen has been injured, stunned," she said. "Help us."

Five days later, the demigod Johann Karlsen, he who had been Carlos Suomi, and Athena Poulson, both of them in fine health, sat at a small table in a corner of what had been the Temple courtyard. Shaded from the midday Hunterian sun by the angle of a ruined wall, they were watching the slave-powered rubble clearing operations making steady progress in the middle distance. There the ship still lay, fifty or sixty meters from the Temple complex, surrounded by a jumble of smashed buildings, where it had come to rest after the drive destroyed itself.

Besides the cultists killed inside the ship or executed by Leros later, at least a score of people, most of them people who had never even known of the berserker's existence, had died in the cataclysm. But still Suomi slept well, for millions of innocent folk across the planet lived and breathed.

"So, Oscar has explained it all to me, finally," Athena announced. "They promised him a chance, a fighting chance, to get at the berserker and destroy it if he cooperated."

"He believed that?"

"He says he knows it was a terribly small chance, but there wasn't any better one. They wouldn't let him get on the ship at all. He just had to sit in a cell and answer questions for Andreas and Lachaise. And the berserker too, it talked to him directly somehow."

"I see." Suomi sipped at his golden goblet of fermented milk. Maybe the stuff made Schoenberg sick, but he had found that his stomach could handle it without difficulty, and he had grown to like the taste.

Athena was looking at him almost dreamily across the little table. "I haven't really had a chance to tell you what I think, Carlos," she said now in a soft, low voice. "It was such a simple idea. Oh, of course I mean simple in the sense of something classical, elegant. And brilliant."

"Hm?"

"The way you used your recordings of Karlsen's voice, and won the battle."

"Oh, well. That was simple, to splice together recorded words to make some phrases that a berserker ought to find appropriately threatening. The main thing was that the berserker should identify his voice and so take the strongest, most violent action it could to kill him, forgetting everything else, be perfectly willing to destroy itself in the process."

"But to conceive of it was brilliant, and to do it required courage."

"Well. When I heard that its servants were asking about Karlsen, for no apparent reason, the idea struck me that we might be dealing with one of those assassin machines, a berserker that had been programmed specifically to go after Karlsen. Even if it was only an ordinary berserker—ha, what am I SAYING?—Karlsen's destruction would rate as a very high priority in its programming, probably higher than de-

populating a minor world. I gambled that it
would just forget its other plans and wreck the
ship, that it would just take it as probable that
Karlsen was somehow hiding on *Orion* with a secret landing party."

"That sounds insane." Then, flustered, Athena tried to modify the implied criticism. "I
mean—"

"It does sound insane. But, as I understand it,
predicting human behavior has never been the
berserkers' strong point. Maybe it thought Andreas had betrayed it after all."

The god Thorun incarnate, who had been
Thomas the Grabber, strolled majestically into
the courtyard at its other end, trailed by priests
and a sculptor who was making sketches for a
new spear-carrying statue. Suomi rose slightly
from his chair and made a little bow in Thorun's
direction. Thorun answered with a smile and a
courteous nod.

Carlos and Thomas understood each other
surprisingly well. The people had to be reassured, society supported, through a time of
crisis. Did Leros and the other devout leaders
really believe that a god and a demigod now
walked among them? Apparently they did, at
least in one compartment of their minds, and at
least as long as such belief suited their needs.
And perhaps in one sense it was the truth that
Karlsen still walked here.

Perhaps, also, the sandy-haired man now
known as Giles the Chancellor, who was
Thorun's constant companion and adviser, was

to a great degree responsible for the relative
smoothness with which the society of Godsmountain had weathered the upheavals of the
past few days. Alas for the Brotherhood. Well,
thought Suomi, likely a world with the Brotherhood victorious would have been no better
than Godsmountain's world was going to be
without its secret demon.

There was Schoenberg now, walking near his
wrecked ship. Barbara Hurtado was at his side
listening to him as he pointed out features of the
rubble-clearing system the slaves were following.
It was a result of his expert analysis of the problem. He had been talking about it yesterday with
Suomi. There, where Schoenberg was now
pointing, was the place where the mathematical-
ly proven plan of greatest efficiency called for all
the debris to be piled. Schoenberg had come
near being killed as a collaborator by Leros and
the winning faction, but intervention by the
demigod Karlsen had saved his life and restored
his freedom.

After what had happened to Celeste Servetus
and Gus De La Torre—their mutilated bodies
had been found atop a small mountain of human
and animal bones in a secret charnel-pit far beneath the Temple—Suomi could not blame
Schoenberg or anyone else for collaboration.
Schoenberg had told him of the tale of ruthless
Earthmen who were going to come looking to
avenge him, a tale that, alas, had been nothing
but pure bluff. Suomi, though, still had the feeling that Schoenberg was leaving something out,
that more had passed between him and Andreas
than he was willing to recount.

Let it lie. The ship had been irreparably damaged, and the surviving members of the hunting expedition were going to have to coexist on this planet, in all likelihood, for an indeterminate number of standard years, until some other ship just happened by.

Athena took a sip of cool water from her fine goblet, and Suomi drank some more fermented milk from his. She had spent the period of crisis locked in her private room and unmolested—maybe she would have been the next day's sacrifice—until the ship crashed and the Temple was knocked down about her ears. Even then she was only shaken up. She, the independent, self-sufficient woman, and by chance she had been forced to sit by passively like some ancient heroine while men fought all around her.

"What are your plans, Carl?"

"I suspect the citizens here will sooner or later get tired of having the demigod Karlsen around, and I just hope it doesn't happen before a ship shows up. I think he'll maintain a low profile, as they say, until then."

"No, I mean Carl Suomi's plans."

"Well." Suddenly he wondered if any of the Hunterians, before the crisis, had heard her call him Carl, as she frequently did. He wondered if that might have contributed to his being so fortunately misidentified. Never mind.

Well. Only a few days ago Carlos Suomi's plans for his future would definitely have included Athena. But that was before he had seen her so avidly viewing men killing each other.

No. Sorry. Of course he himself had now killed more people than she had even seen die—

yet in a real sense he was still a pacifist, more so than ever in fact, and she was not. That was how he saw the matter, anyway.

Barbara, now. She was still standing beside Schoenberg as he lectured her, but she looked over from time to time toward the place where Suomi sat. Suomi wanted nice things to happen to Barbara. Last night she had shared his bed. The two of them had laughed about their minor injuries, comparing bruises. But . . . a playgirl. No. His life would go on just about the same if he never saw Barbara again.

What, then, were his plans, as Athena put it? Well, there were plenty of other fish splashing in the seas of Earth, or even, if he could be allowed a mangled metaphor, living demure and veiled behind their white walls here on Godsmountain. He still wanted a woman, and in more ways than one.

Schoenberg was now pointing up into the sky. Would his rubble pile grow that tall? Then Barbara leaped with excitement, and Suomi looked up and saw the ship.

Next thing they were all running, shouting, looking for the emergency radios that Schoenberg had insisted on getting from the *Orion* and keeping handy. Some trying-to-be-helpful Hunterian had misplaced the radios. Never mind. The ship lowered rapidly, drawn by the beacon-like appearance of the city atop the mountain, and *Orion* already sitting there. A silvery sphere, similar in every way to Schoenberg's craft. With wild waves Earthmen and Hunterians beckoned it to land on a cleared spot amid the rubble.

Landing struts out and down, drive off, hatch open, landing ramp extruded. A tall man emerging, with the pallor of one probably raised under a dome on Venus, his long mustache waxed and shaped in the form the Earth-descended Venerians frequently affected. Reassured by numerous signs of friendly welcome, he strode halfway down the ramp, putting on sunglasses against the Hunterian noon. "How do, folks, Steve Kemalchek, Venus. Say, what happened here, an earthquake?"

Thorun and the High Priest Leros were still deciding which of them should make the official welcoming speech. Suomi moved a little closer to the ramp and said informally: "Something like that. But things are under control now."

The man looked relieved on hearing the familiar accents of an Earthman's speech. "You're from Earth, right? That's your ship. Get any hunting in yet? I've just been up north, got a stack of trophy 'grams in there . . . show you later." He lowered his voice to a more confidential tone. "And, say, is that Tournament everything I've heard it is? Going on right now, ain't it? Isn't this the place?"

BESTSELLING
Science Fiction
and
Fantasy

☐ 47810-7	**THE LEFT HAND OF DARKNESS,** Ursula K. Le Guin	$2.95
☐ 16022-0	**DORSAI!,** Gordon R. Dickson	$2.95
☐ 80584-1	**THIEVES' WORLD,**™ Robert Lynn Asprin, editor	$2.95
☐ 11452-0	**CONAN #1,** Robert E. Howard, L. Sprague de Camp, Lin Carter	$2.95
☐ 49142-1	**LORD DARCY INVESTIGATES,** Randall Garrett	$2.75
☐ 87330-8	**THE WARLOCK UNLOCKED,** Christopher Stasheff	$2.95
☐ 05490-0	**BERSERKER,** Fred Saberhagen	$2.95
☐ 10264-6	**CHANGELING,** Roger Zelazny	$2.95
☐ 51554-1	**THE MAGIC GOES AWAY,** Larry Niven	$2.95

Prices may be slightly higher in Canada.

Available at your local bookstore or return this form to:

ACE SCIENCE FICTION
Book Mailing Service
P.O. Box 690, Rockville Centre, NY 11571

Please send me the titles checked above. I enclose _____ Include 75¢ for postage and handling if one book is ordered; 25¢ per book for two or more not to exceed $1.75. California, Illinois, New York and Tennessee residents please add sales tax.

NAME _____

ADDRESS _____

CITY _____ STATE/ZIP _____

(allow six weeks for delivery)   SF 9